CODEX SILENDA:
The Apprentice and the Secret Labyrinth

BRAD JEFFERSON

Cover design by Petar Denkov

Copyright © 2017 Brad Jefferson
Northern Lights, Camera, Action Productions, LLC

ISBN: 978-1-521896-20-4

Inspired and based on the concept from:

Codex Silenda: The Book of Puzzles
(www.CodexSilenda.com)

By
Brady Whitney

For Vivian

whose love, unconditional support,
and endless patience serve as my inspiration.

CONTENTS

Acknowledgments	i
Preface	iii
Discovery	1
Journal	4
Chapter 1 - Learning from the Master	6
Chapter 2 - Finding an Apprentice	13
Chapter 3 - The Interview	29
Chapter 4 - The First Day	41
Chapter 5 - Training and Learning	58
Chapter 6 - Shadow Dancing	73
Chapter 7 - The Squabble	82
Chapter 8 - The Trip	91
Chapter 9 - Exposing Secrets	96
Chapter 10 - From Plan into Action	99
Chapter 11 - Into the Darkness	106
Chapter 12 - Mending Fences and The Guest	126
Chapter 13 - The Geneva Wheel	133
Chapter 14 - The Never-Ending Path	144
Chapter 15 - The Paradox Sliders	147
Chapter 16 - The Cryptex	157
Chapter 17 - Consequences	178
Chapter 18 - Spectra	187
Epilogue: Koda Khronika	200
Headline News (Present Day)	224
Revelation, Reflection, and Beauty	227
About the Author	232

Brad Jefferson

ACKNOWLEDGMENTS

"No duty is more urgent than that of returning thanks."
-- James Allen

Thank you to my copyeditor, Lisa Zahn ("writerlisaz" from www.Fiverr.com) and my beta readers/editors for their valuable insight and encouragement: Cherie, Brenda Curkendall, Thuan Cook, and Robert Peesel.

Thank you to the artistic talents of Petar Denkov, Maurizio Simonini, Marlena Kostrzewska, Paul Talib Bhajjan, and Abi Daker who provided beautiful Italian Renaissance-style sketches and drawings for this story. From the Fiverr.com artists for their contributions: Tay Chin Siong (Sunnypixels), Rozmarina, and Azureprince.

Thank you, Brady Whitney. You provided the initial seed of inspiration by creating the Codex Silenda puzzle book. Your energetic level of creativity, out-of-the-box artistic talent, and mechanical game theory put you as a genius in my book any day.

And my family. Thank you to Vivian and Natalie for your patience while the original short story grew into a larger project. Your encouragement and initial reviews helped me become a better storyteller. Thank you to my son Kevin and to Nadia Ghosheh for your valuable insight into the Latin world for translating words and concepts into meaningful phrases used within the story. All of you have stood by my side and supported everything I do.

Special thanks to my mom, who provided reviews and insightful comments. I love you, Mom. Now, get back to those walks in the woods.

This short story is dedicated to all writers and visionaries who have the energy and passion to try something new. Don't let anyone say you can't do it. Challenge yourself and go forth with a passion.

"Agite Excelsius!"
("Go to a place higher up,
accomplish even greater things!")

PREFACE

On August 11, 2016, I received an email titled "This Week in Kickstarter" from Kickstarter.com, which highlighted several new projects under its helm. Kickstarter is a large crowd funding platform for helping bring creative projects to life. One project was titled "Codex Silenda: The Book of Puzzles" by Brady Whitney.

The concept was described as "this wooden, laser-cut puzzle book that features five unique, intricately designed riddles. The catch: the only way to unlock each 'page' is by solving the puzzle before it." The Kickstarter pages went into further detail:

> *"As the puzzler moves through the book, a story begins to unfold, depicting the story of an apprentice in Da Vinci's Workshop who encounters the same Codex. However, in the story, the Codex acts as a trap set by Da Vinci to capture any would be spies/snoopy apprentices in order to protect his work. The only way to escape is to solve each of the puzzles before the Master returns from his trip."*

Wow. I was immediately mesmerized and quite fascinated at this creative and unique puzzle. I thought the puzzle could be the stimulus and springboard into a short story, or screenplay, or even a movie. My mind was creatively invigorated from all directions. I was re-minded of the books and movies for **National Treasure**, **Jumanji**, and even the 1982 TV show **Voyagers!** Could the five pages of this intriguing wooden puzzle book be adapted into a fictional tale, an adventure of a young apprentice?

I wrote Brady Whitney that day with my thoughts and ideas. I shared with him the potential for taking his creation onto a new creative page. I told him that when the dust settled on his Kickstarter campaign, he should get back to me and we could discuss it further.

Brady responded to me 35 minutes later (the wonders of the Internet and email) and said, "Wow, I never quite thought of the Codex being considered part of a screenplay, but I definitely like the sound of it!" He told me that, "With a collaborative effort, I could certainly see a short story unfolding as a short film. I will certainly be interested in discussing this further after the campaign has ended." The game was afoot, so to speak.

The Kickstarter campaign was a tremendous success. Having been funded in a record six hours, Brady's focus immediately went toward producing this puzzle for his Kickstarter backers.

In later correspondence, Brady provided me the story that would appear on each of the puzzle pages. Each of the chapters in his story described and provided clues for how the apprentice was to solve that puzzle. I started on an outline, integrating Brady's material with my ideas. This progressed naturally into the story you see here.

I hope you enjoy reading **Codex Silenda: The Apprentice and the Secret Labyrinth**, but do not miss the chance to play, solve, and immerse yourself into Brady Whitney's puzzle, **Codex Silenda: The Book of Puzzles**.

BRAD JEFFERSON

DISCOVERY

A recent archaeological excavation in the city of Florence, Italy has revealed fascinating insights into the life of Leonardo da Vinci. The unearthed objects include paintings, sketches, and a large volume of written material – all in near-excellent condition. These artifacts present a new perspective of Leonardo da Vinci's persona as well as the challenges and adventures of three young people who were apprenticed to him.

What is known about the great Master is based on his documented manuscripts and notebooks. Leonardo da Vinci's achievements made him a leading figure in the Italian Renaissance; his inventions changed the world. The artifact discovery complements this knowledge with a set of journals by one of the apprentices that provide detailed accounts of the elaborate lengths Leonardo went through to protect his inventions and artistic works-in-progress.

Understanding the full meaning and context of these archaeological treasures required a highly skilled team of scientists. Renowned archaeologist Rubera Bostaurusini and her team were commissioned to examine the site, and to describe, classify, translate, and identify these artifacts.

Archaeological Notes on the Text and Translation

The following sections include text translated from the Florentine Italian and Latin journals and manuscripts of Francesco Andrea Aiello, an apprentice of Leonardo da Vinci.

When translating these entries, the Bostaurusini Archaeological Team, in cooperation with the *Museo archeologico nazionale di Firenze*[1], has attempted to keep as close to the entries as possible while remaining consistent with readable English, and while also capturing something of the flavor of Francesco Andrea Aiello's varied style.

---

[1] Museo archeologico nazionale di Firenze → National Archaeological Museum of Florence, Italy.

Many words or phrases were not translated. Those items are denoted with a footnote and their definition is provided at the bottom of the page. There are several references on the Internet that provide full etymology and pronunciation for these Italian and Latin concepts.

The measurement unit for length used in Florence during this time period (1400s-1500s) and identified in the journals was the _braccio_[2]. For standardization purposes, all references herein to this measurement have been converted to the metric system's: meter. For conversion purposes, 1 _braccio_ = 0.583 meters or 1.9 feet.

Original Journal Sketches and Drawings

Sketches and drawings from Aiello's manuscripts and journals are included in this text as they were originally found in the archaeological discovery. Each item has been carefully stabilized, preserved, and repaired during the archaeological conservation effort.

---

[2] Braccio → An old Italian unit of length.

JOURNAL

We live in a small two bedroom house just outside of *Porta San Pier Gattolino*[3], in the southern part of *Repubblica Fiorentina*[4] in Tuscany. I live with my Papa and Momma, my brother Niccolo, and my sister Serena. My parents provide a roof over our heads, food for our mouths, and love for us to make it from one day to the next.

We are a strong, hardworking family. We help each other out, treat everyone with respect, learn to compromise, never break a promise, and learn to forgive.

The eighth of March is a special day; it is my birthday. The year I turned fourteen, I received a very special gift from Momma. She had made me a leather-bound journal to keep a

---

[3] Porta San Pier Gattolino → Now known as Porta Romana, the southernmost gate in the 13th-century walls of the Oltrarno section of Florence, region of Tuscany, Italy.

[4] Repubblica Fiorentina → Republic of Florence.

personal record of my life, events, and experiences, and a place for my sketches and drawings. Engraved on its supple, brown leather cover was my name:

Francesco Andrea Aiello

Momma has always guided me throughout my life and encourages me to appreciate everything and everyone. This journal and subsequent volumes are my record, my personal chronicle, of those life experiences.

The following story is a recount over the course of a year of a special time where my friends and I were fortunate to be the receivers of unexpected and certainly extraordinary events. These situations occurred either by pure luck or divine intervention. During this time, in hindsight, it seemed like everything fell into place in an unusual yet exhilarating way.

I had made decisions on which paths to take and learned from many mistakes along the way. Over the year that transpired, those experiences led me to make choices that allowed me to understand the life I was intended to live and to establish a solid foundation for an exciting future.

This all started with my pencil, paper, and a passion.

CHAPTER 1 - LEARNING FROM THE MASTER

The unforgiving and continuous rainstorm pounded the shingles on our roof. Sometimes water dripped on top of my desk and papers, but today I was lucky; there were no leaks, not a drop. It wasn't a big desk, but it was large enough for me to draw and sketch designs in my journal. Often, I retreated here to escape the distractions of my brother and sister.

Today's rain masked all other noises and helped me concentrate on my latest project, one of Florence's architectural masterpieces, the *Il Duomo di Firenze*[5]. This large, breath-taking cathedral had a beautiful, red-tiled masonry dome. Unlike most domes, this was octagonal rather than round, with distinctive

---

[5] Il Duomo di Firenze → Also known as Cattedrale di Santa Maria del Fiore.

marble panels in various shades of green and pink.

I was baptized in the cathedral several years after it was built. That was my first introduction to the beautiful and ornate structures around Florence, though I don't remember the specific details from that time as I was preoccupied with being a crying infant. The cathedral was dedicated to Santa Maria del Fiore, the Virgin of the Flower. The *Fleur-de-Lys*[6] is a recognized symbol of Florence and cannot be ignored as you walk around the city and view its many decorative monuments.

My two favorite flowers are the lily and the iris. Each flower had its unique and stunning

---

[6] Fleur-de-Lys → Flower of the lily.

beauty. Varieties of lily symbolize purity, beauty, modesty, virginity, and passion. The iris represents power and majesty, with the three petal segments representing faith, wisdom, and valor. Momma taught me to appreciate beauty in everything and be happy with my God-given talents. I just needed to discover what those talents were.

She taught us to appreciate everything in life; to treasure nature and God's gift of birds, animals, flowers, the outdoors, and blue skies; and, to embrace the inherent love in people. Beauty was all around us and in many different forms. We just needed to open our eyes to see it.

During the summer months, Momma always displayed a bouquet of flowers on our dinner table to brighten up our house. When in season, the bouquet included beautiful purple irises and multi-colored lilies. Though Papa instilled in me a sense of honor and a spirit of determination and dedication, it was Momma who helped nurture and cultivate my interests, and helped shape the person I am today.

As I got older, Momma and Papa introduced me to new and different activities to challenge myself. My parents wanted to raise

Niccolo, Serena, and me to be healthy and educated young adults – and to enjoy whatever we set our hearts out to do.

One phrase of wisdom Momma said to me when I was six or seven has stayed with me ever since, "There is not one path. There is not even the right path. There is only your path."

As a result, my interests grew in several directions, like swimming, rock collecting, writing, and even more, drawing. I was attracted to sketching and drawing almost anything: flowers, bugs, scenery, and people. The more I drafted images on paper, the more disciplined I became in thinking, planning, setting aside time away from sibling distractions, and establishing goals. I had always been able to see the big picture in my mind as well as give attention to the smallest detail. I was fascinated with measurements and angles. And I enjoyed the challenge to analyze and critically assess problems. My focus quickly narrowed toward architectural drawing.

My path led me to a wonderful life experience and adventure I could never imagine: to be an apprentice for the great Leonardo di ser Piero da Vinci. We simply called him Leonardo.

Leonardo's studio was located immediately outside the city of Florence. He was a man of many passions, a great thinker and a genius, who discovered many fundamental principles.

To say Leonardo was a man of many artistic and scientific disciplines would be an understatement. He was a painter, draftsman, sculptor, architect, and engineer. His talents were fed by his superb intellect, his heightened sense of curiosity, and a desire for knowledge. At least, that was what my close friends and I thought of him firsthand, as we were Leonardo's first apprentices.

For Leonardo to know the world as he did was truly amazing. To question everything that was known and to conceptualize and visualize the world with different eyes and a different vision, was to dream and turn the unimaginable into the possible. There were rules that defined why the things in our world acted the way they did and why they did not. Leonardo discovered these rules, principles, and fundamental truths about reality — and threw out precepts that had no foundation in the universe.

Everything had boundaries — just not the boundaries we currently understood or believed. Leonardo saw beyond current reality and physical limitations and understood their importance or significance for his world. What he considered visionary, innovative, and straightforward, others criticized as insane and invalid. This made Leonardo an eccentric; his mind and personality seemed to us as super-human, the man himself mysterious and remote. In his mind, the world was alive with fantastic possibilities. But in the world around him, he was somewhat lonely.

This, I believed, was his motive to share what he knew. His aspiration was to find young, uninfluenced individuals through apprenticeships, those who had the potential to think like he did, to challenge the impossible, to release their imagination, and to dream beyond what was. It was his goal to teach others how to see and apply creativity to every aspect of their lives.

As Leonardo was a prodigious visionary, he was also mysterious. He employed non-traditional techniques with his art, experiments, and observations. Possibly logical and well-thought-out in his mind, some of these methods were contrary to what was usual, traditional, or accepted for his time. And ever so much, that was what I admired about him; he reached beyond and asked, "Why not?" There was so much I learned from Leonardo and his outlook on life.

Leonardo's passion reached beyond the beautiful and serene. Some of his inventions, though incredibly complex and intricate, yet sometimes simplistic looking, could be used as powerful weapons — military weapons. They could be destructive if they landed into the wrong hands. This caused frequent concern for Leonardo. He was very protective of his notes, his sketches — basically everything. We noticed this daily when we worked in his studio. Leonardo may have been a bit paranoid as he often hid secret codes and messages in his artwork. He was an overprotective mother of his creations.

As an architect, I was extremely naive and inexperienced. My world was limited to what I knew. And at the age of fourteen, it wasn't very much when measured against Leonardo's talents. In retrospect, my skills as a designer were unsophisticated and unrefined. So what went through my mind and enticed me to apply to become his apprentice? What would Leonardo see in me?

CHAPTER 2 - FINDING AN APPRENTICE

One day when Momma was at the market talking with her friends, she found out that an artist, Leonardo da Vinci, was looking to hire an apprentice. Two apprentices, to be exact. She immediately relayed that news to me as she knew I was ready to take the next step. I just didn't know that I was ready.

I had seen some of his paintings and frescoes. I admired his choice of color palette, using natural hues that were muted in intensity. I saw the complexity in his paintings, the intense thought that went into achieving depth and character with every brush stroke. His method was very similar to how I approached architectural drawing – with a distinct attention and passion for detail.

I frequently stayed up late sketching the places I had visited earlier in the day: the buildings and offices near the piazza; the stalls of the town merchants; the many ornate, beautiful gilded churches whose colorful stained glass windows and tall columns accentuated and decorated their sacred interiors; the medieval stone arch bridge, Ponte Vecchio, at the corner of town; and even our small two bedroom house.

Niccolo was a sound sleeper and I didn't have to worry about waking him up when I worked and drafted at my desk. Though he was only two years younger than I, we were very different. While I stayed up late and woke early, Niccolo enjoyed any chance to sleep. And sometimes in the morning, I found he had stolen the covers during the night, leaving me cold and annoyed.

Serena had slept in Momma and Papa's room since she was born. At eight years old, Serena was still small enough for me to enjoy carrying her on my shoulders when we went on our frequent visits to the market. She rested her head on mine while we walked, with her straggly hair floating in front of my face. I walked haphazardly, swerving left and right and bobbing up and down, having fun with her, pretending I couldn't see where I was going. Then I would blow her hair away from my nose and she would giggle. I enjoyed our trips into town.

Niccolo and Serena were dear to my heart. I was their big brother and took it upon myself to set an example for them and be a role model, someone they could look up to for advice.

In the early mornings, Serena often ran into our bedroom to wake Niccolo and me. Even though she was half our weight and size, Serena climbed on our bed and jumped up and down, bouncing off Niccolo's legs or my feet. We playfully wrestled with her until she settled down. We loved Serena dearly, but wished she would give us an extra hour of rest before her exuberant wakeup call challenged our peaceful slumber.

Every so often around mid-morning, Momma would request the services of the Aiello Fishing Company, the fun name Niccolo, Serena, and I gave ourselves as an excuse to go fishing. We enjoyed strolling along the banks of the river to catch fish. Niccolo and I were innovative fishermen with makeshift poles, line, lures, and bait. And importantly, we knew the right fishing holes along the winding river where we could catch many fish, though we were not in any hurry as we always enjoyed relaxing, chatting, and wading in the waters.

Sometimes on warm summer days, we laid back on the river bank and let our fishing poles linger in the calm flowing waters, waiting for the fish to take the bait. When Serena got bored, she often surprised us with a splash of cool water on our faces—which scared the fish away. Interestingly, as soon as she was tired out, the fished returned and took nibbles from our lines.

A couple of years earlier, when the Aiello Fishing Company was returning from a day's fishing expedition, I met Leonardo da Vinci for the first time.

We had been fishing and were carrying back two large and two small catfish. The smaller fish tasted much better, but today we were lucky and found all the right fishing spots; we didn't want to throw back any fish. As a result, our load was heavy.

Niccolo and I fashioned netting that was hooked onto our long wooden fishing rods to carry the fish home. Serena carried our bucket of bait and snacks. Momma packed some fresh bread, grapes, and apples for when we got hungry. Fishing was hard work at our age.

We talked about how Momma would prepare dinner later that day after I filleted the catch. Would she make her *zuppa di pesce*[7] or her fish fry? There was nothing like fresh fish for dinner.

As we walked along the banks of the Arno River with its broad olive waters, between the *colonnades*[8] and *campaniles*[9] of Florence, we came

---

[7] <u>Zuppa di pesce</u> → Fish soup with fish or seafood and vegetables.

across a man walking in the opposite direction. His hair was long and blond, but looked dirty and messed up by the wind. His eyes were a soft friendly blue. His clothes were marked with dark black streaks, similar to how Serena looked when she came in from playing in the dirt.

As we sat down to rest our arms from the load of fish, the man also stopped. He said his name was Leonardo da Vinci. His voice had a warm, pleasant, and gentle tone.

---

[8] Colonnades → A row of tall columns that support a building or a roof.

[9] Campaniles → A freestanding bell tower.

He complimented us on our impressive catch. I noticed he carried a satchel and that his hands were black and his clothing smelled like gunpowder. He had been busy earlier in the day.

Leonardo talked to us about his love for water. How it worked, how it flowed and moved, and how it could be diverted to control floods or commerce.

We ate our snacks and listened further. "Water is the driving force of all nature," he said, and told us about his visions of different ways of traveling over water in a paddle boat. He described the technology to possibly power the boat more efficiently.

His explanations were fascinating, and I thought he was fascinating. Niccolo and Serena did not understand a word he said and kept munching on the snacks Momma provided.

His talk with us was very open and friendly. However, I was only ten years old at the time, and I did not know what was impossible. I took his statements as something that could be.

Leonardo said he had come back from a farm where he tested a new type of gun. Niccolo and Serena put down their food and shifted closer to the discussion. Leonardo pulled out a drawing for what he called a *ribauldequin*[10] and explained, "We were successful in our tests today. The gun is different from others. As you can see there are several horizontal barrels connected together like a fan." He pointed out various parts of the gun from the drawing.

After studying the picture for a few moments, Serena commented, "That looks like our pipe organ in church."

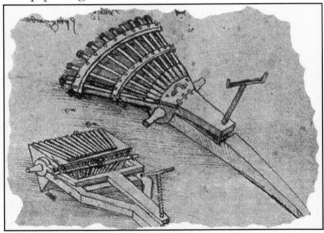

Niccolo laughed and nudged her in the arm, "Yes, but I bet it sounds a lot different."

---

[10] <u>Ribauldequin</u> → A late medieval volley gun with many small-caliber iron barrels set up parallel on a platform. When the gun was fired in a volley, it created a shower of iron shot.

Leonardo said he tested many different designs and this latest trial run proved very successful. But he cautioned, "This is not a toy; it is a tool of battle."

As serious as he seemed throughout our talk with him, Leonardo frequently sniffed his darkened hands and breathed deep. It seemed like he loved the smell of gunpowder.

A call of thunder sounded from the distance. I knew we should be getting back home soon. Momma would be worried.

Leonardo looked over at some of the sketches I had lying on the grass. "I see you are an artist. May I take a look?"

I handed him one of my drawings. He handled it very carefully so as not to smear any of the pencil.

"Nice. Very nice. I like how you captured your siblings fishing and enjoying themselves. Nice facial reactions and perspective. Yes, very nice. You have a gift. Keep at it." He felt several drops of rain land on his face and handed me back the drawing.

"Yes, sir, I will."

He shook each of our hands and bid us farewell.

As the skies opened up with a torrent of rain, we quickly packed up our gear and headed home. I hadn't seen Leonardo again since that first meeting.

Though he was described by my friends as a bit strange and eccentric, I sensed something unique and special about him. By the way he talked, Leonardo presented a complex topic in a way I could understand.

That first meeting was years ago, when I was young and inexperienced. I am older now and have grown to better understand how to take my ideas and transform them into architectural designs.

My life was divided between activities with my family, daily chores, my girlfriend Giovanna Bronzino, and my passion for drawing. Every morning, if not awakened by Serena, I rose early to feed the chickens and clean their coops. I made sure no predators like dogs, cats, or rats could disturb the chicken's roost or make their way through the fence. Though if they did, our rooster would help guard and protect his hens by alerting them to impending danger. Niccolo and Serena's chore was to collect any eggs the hens laid that day.

After those tasks, Niccolo, Serena, and I would join Momma on trips to the farmers market to get fresh produce and meat. She gave us specific duties: Niccolo and Serena would collect fresh greens and potatoes; I would pick up milk, butter, and cheeses.

Several days of the week, I would spend a lot of time with Giovanna wandering around town and meeting up with our friends. We both enjoyed getting together at our church socials; listening to music, singing, and dancing most Sunday afternoons; and just sitting alone together.

Though Giovanna and I enjoyed singing church music and hymns, we looked forward to singing our favorite *frottola*[11] songs. These were simple, easily singable songs suited for our amateur voices. Usually they were love songs from a popular poem. Giovanna and I created beautiful harmony.

The church provided us a popular venue to have fun with the younger kids, though Giovanna was the real star. She set up a small stage made up of two chairs, with a curtain made from colorful pieces of fabric. When she was ready she would put on one of her many handmade puppets and begin her show. Giovanna constructed each puppet out of leather and wire. Each animal, anatomically accurate with its wings, legs, and head, came to life through the articulated movement of her fingers, hands, and the sounds from her voice. Her favorite puppet was a cute bird she called *Pulcino*[12].

---

[11] Frottola → A special kind of popular song usually made up of a simple melody and based on any number of poetic forms, often driven by a love theme.

[12] Pulcino → A baby chicken.

Giovanna as the master puppeteer, and I as her understudy with a sock hand puppet, would entertain the children with little skits and humorous plays. The young audience loved watching us bring the innovative and animated puppets to life. I loved being with her as we shared these fun moments together.

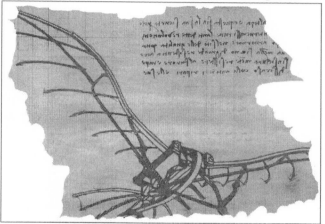

Afterwards, we would dance in the church hall to a variety of instrumental music. Giovanna and I enjoyed these gatherings. It was her outlet to share her passion with others. She was my closest friend and became my beloved companion.

Giovanna and I grew up in the same neighborhood. Her parents and older sister were good friends with my family. Both our families were involved at the church and often had picnics in the park together.

She had the most beautiful, long flowing hair and dark brown, mysterious eyes that gazed at me when I wasn't looking. She had always been my favorite person to hang around and we had so much fun.

When we were younger, we often played *Lupo Mangia Frutta*[13] with the other kids in our neighborhood. This is where a kid was chosen to be the wolf, who then walked twenty paces away and covered his ears. The other children clustered together and each one selected a different kind of fruit to be, such as apple, mango, etc. Once they all agreed, all of the "fruits" stood together in a line opposite the wolf. The wolf then said, "Knock, knock," and all the fruit asked, "Who is it?" The wolf would reply, "I am the fruit-eating wolf," and the other children would call out, "What fruit do you want?" The wolf called out the name of a fruit. If one of the children playing had chosen to be that fruit, that child must run away from the wolf, who tried to chase them. If the wolf succeeded, then that child was the wolf in the next round, and if not, then the wolf had

---

[13] <u>Lupo Mangia Frutta</u> → Fruit-eating wolf.

another turn — until all the fruits were caught and eaten by the wolf.

Giovanna always picked grapes because she loved their sweet, delicate flavor. When I was caught and became the wolf, I would try and leave my "grape" guess near the end of the game so I wouldn't get Giovanna upset. We played for hours until it was time for dinner.

Now, when I am at home and things settle down for the evening, my attention changes. I pull out my paper and pencil and unleash my creativity. My initial designs were certainly imaginative and original, and were at least somewhat accomplished through my eyes. When I look at those drawings, I see a part of me, my soul, in their creation. That makes me feel remarkable. I wanted architecture to be an important part of my future, but I needed to develop better skills.

An apprenticeship with Leonardo would give me the opportunity to learn from a master. I needed to transform this unique artistic emotion of mine into a lifelong career. I wanted to be a celebrated virtuoso of architecture whose creations were viewed and admired all around town. Leonardo da Vinci could make that happen for me.

That is, if I was chosen as his apprentice. Would he remember our meeting at the river years ago? Was I that prodigy, that young artist who was gifted with the exceptional qualities and abilities he was looking for? I would never know unless I took that next step.

CHAPTER 3 - THE INTERVIEW

After a strong thunderstorm overnight, Saturday morning fared better as the sun peeked through the scattering clouds. I walked through the piazza toward Leonardo's studio to interview for the apprenticeship. Between dodging puddles of water left from the storm, I noticed patches of beautiful, pale turquoise blue that emerged from the clouded sky. As I crested the hill near the piazza, the horizon cleared up and I could see for miles in every direction.

I took with me my portfolio of selected designs and sketches. I was sure Leonardo would think those would be important to see. They were my best pieces of work, inspired by the Roman architecture that filled me with wonder.

A couple of summers ago, my father and I traveled to Rome and visited the Colosseum for a religious event. Centered in Rome, the

elliptical amphitheater was a stunning architectural feat. As we watched from the second
tier seating, I pulled out my scroll and sketched
many of the building's features, including the
monumental open arcades and wide marble
terraces. My father mentioned that years
before, each of the Colosseum's arches contained a statue made from clay or marble.
Those statues had since vanished.

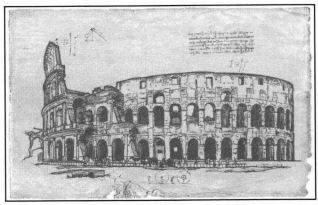

I admired the variety of column styles on
each of the floors, but unfortunately, the structure was crumbling away in places. If I were to
design such a massive and iconic structure, I
would make sure it lasted for a millennia.

I brought several of my Colosseum
drawings with me for the interview. I carried
my portfolio with pride and gratification,

awaiting to share my accomplishments with the Master.

For good luck, I walked past the storm-water drain grate that Leonardo da Vinci designed for the town years ago. It was an elaborate system used to prevent flooding in parts of town. I tossed a few coins through the slots in the grate for extra luck. As kids, we threw pebbles down for fun, but today I was looking for an advantage — as much luck as I could get.

As I continued my walk, I noticed more and more young men were heading in the same direction. We stopped outside of Leonardo's studio. The building had a beautiful *Terra di Siena*[14] color. Several houses in our village used this same clay soil from the Tuscany region, which had that alluring brownish pigment. I included some of those sketches in my portfolio.

On top of his building, there were two small glass cupolas integrated into the roof structure, one on each side of the sloped roof. Each of the domes' sizes seemed about half a

---

[14] Terra di Siena → "Siena earth" is an earth pigment containing iron oxide and manganese oxide. In its natural state, it is yellow-brown.

meter wide in diameter and less than a third of a meter tall. From an architectural point of view, they looked spectacular. And based on their size, I imagined it was difficult and technically challenging for the glass maker to create such a piece.

On the far side of the rooftop, there was a strange, spiral-shaped device that rotated when the wind changed directions. This must have been an invention that Leonardo da Vinci created. These devices were fascinating to look at and piqued my curiosity as to their purpose.

I glanced down to the street level to see that there was a line with some twenty other prospective apprentices. The more candidates who interviewed, the smaller my chances for selection. Though initially confident that I would get the job, my dream was darkened before I even got inside the door. There were others here who probably had talents way beyond my capabilities. As I waited, several more people showed up behind me. My heart sunk even more. I knew that the artistic, youthful talents of Florence and its surrounding towns were impressive. I just hadn't planned to be dispirited so soon into the morning.

Slowly, the candidates walked up the stairs toward the studio. As I waited my turn in a long, dark hallway, each person moved like a worm, inching himself slowly forward across the floor. The hall-way walls were covered in beautiful, yet only partially completed, frescoes and sketches of birds. As one candidate finished inter-viewing and left the studio, we each moved forward one step.

As I got closer to the door, the floor's long, splintered wooden planks tran-sitioned into a beautiful circular, symmetrical pattern on the floor. Through one small window in the hallway, small rays of sun high-lighted lavender colored flowers, integrated into the intricate, five-paneled spiral design. The hypnotizing pattern sent me back to when my family visited the Giardino dell'Iris gardens in Florence.

We admired the beautiful spectrum of iris flowers each spring, offering a color spectacle second to none. I wish I was able to experience this colorful exhibition in all seasons of the year. Those flowers must have been his inspiration for this beautiful floor design.

Leonardo had created beauty in the most unexciting and unusual locations. I saw that art and architecture could be reflected everywhere. Not only for walls, or pedestals, or outside buildings, but now floors. Any location could be an inviting canvas waiting to be born. Although the floor's design was a warm welcome to Leonardo's *atelier*[15], apprehension and nervousness flowed through my body.

In quick turn, I was next. As I stood there in front of the door, waiting for my fate to reveal itself, I wondered whether I could I show him how skillful and artistic I was. What questions would he ask and would I know the answer? Exactly how do you talk with a master who knows everything?

---

[15] Atelier → A workshop or studio, especially one used by an artist or designer.

Through the door, I heard the legs of a chair scrape against a wooden floor. Then two locks on the door turned. Why lock the door? What could be inside that room that obligated securing this door from a line of innocent, young, would-be apprentices? Wouldn't closing the door be enough?

The door opened and a young man with a withdrawn look of despair exited. He wasn't happy or sad. I heard a monotone voice call out, "Next." I looked at the person behind me and then looked forward as I took a few steps into the room. The door closed behind me and I heard the locks go back into their secure position.

A man with long curly hair, carefully styled, and a short beard hurried past me. He wore a short, rose-colored tunic that went down to his knees. Nervously, I gazed as he rounded the desk and sat down. Leonardo da Vinci was like I had remembered him.

Though I was still somewhat tense, to ease my trepidation, I smiled at him. "*Buongiorno*[16]. Sit down or stand. This won't take long," he spoke in a monotone voice. I moved toward the chair and grasped its top knob. I slowly sat

---

[16] Buongiorno → Good morning.

down and awaited his next command. "What is your name?"

I answered innocently, "Francesco Aiello of Florence."

With my eyes fixed straight at him, Leonardo looked at me and then directly past, peering at the wall. His focus apparently wandered as he circled around the room. He ambled to the window and spoke, "A beautiful day, isn't it? The clouds and sky, friendly companions in a calm and peaceful world."

I didn't know what to say. Trying to conjure up a respectable response, I answered with the best, most intelligent reply I could muster, "Yes."

He pivoted toward me and inquired, "Now, what is your artistic passion?"

I answered nervously, "I like to design things. Architecture fascinates me and drives me to create."

Leonardo returned to the desk. "Yes, that's good. But what drives that passion? What motivates you to put those ideas on paper? Do you follow any special rules? How do you frame your thoughts?"

I didn't know what he wanted to hear. I thought about some of the drawings I had done recently, staying up into the late hours at my desk. I held my portfolio even closer to me. I cleared my throat. "I feel joy in creating and designing. My imagination is alive in me when I do. I experience peace and relaxation when I express myself freely. I see the world as my inspiration."

"Ah-ha, yes. Go ahead. Tell me more."

"These ideas, they are beautiful and they are real. Every town needs a bridge. People need a place to sleep and work. I would like to design those things."

Leonardo looked down at the portfolio on my lap, "Let me see what you brought." I opened the thin, simple leather case and took out my drawings and sketches, and placed them on his desk next to a bundle of scrolls. A small cloud of dust swirled into the air, particles slowly lingering as if they were a flock of birds aloft, enjoying a warm August breeze.

Leonardo picked up each page and looked intently at each part of the drawing. There was no expression on his face. "Hmm, I've seen this style before. It's okay." He finished looking at the rest of the drawings and handed the stack back to me. I placed the papers back into my portfolio. I had failed. He was not impressed.

Solemnly, I continued, "I am sorry. I do not know the rules of great architecture. I have wasted your time." I stood up and proceeded toward the door.

As I reached for the door latch, he exclaimed, "STOP!" I immediately froze in my steps. "Simplicity is the ultimate sophistication. What you have done in these drawings is good. They could be a lot better." I turned around and looked at him, my face directed down to the floor. He asked, "Are these what you had first imagined? Did they come from your heart?"

I looked up at him and answered with a relaxed, confident reply, "Yes, they are, sir."

He stood up and approached me. In a calm chuckle, he whispered, "I like simple answers." He placed his hand on my shoulder. "Architecture is a visual art, and the buildings speak for themselves. Everything we do must have a unique, distinct character that we give to everything we create. We give it life. A spirit that comes from within us. That is what I am looking for in an apprentice."

I looked at Leonardo with a bit of confusion. He lifted his hand from my shoulder and stepped to the door. He whispered, "There are two primary tenets that must be applied when you create. The first is knowing the fundamental principles of the craft. You must know light and shadows, angles and textures, balance and variety, and much more."

Much of what Leonardo said made sense. I felt disappointed that the interview was over and that I had not convinced him of my full potential. Was this advice an important lesson from which I could become a better architect? I asked in a soft-spoken voice, "What is the second tenet?"

"The second and most important is: You can follow the rules, but if you don't create from your heart, then 'you' have not created ... art. Without giving it a soul and spirit, the results are just colors on a canvas, textures on a sculpture, and lines on paper."

He started to unlock the door and continued quietly, "As one of my apprentices ..." What did my ears hear? In a delighted shock, I looked at him ever more intensely. "... you will start your work with me the day after next, one hour after sunrise. You will be paid at the end of each week."

I was thrilled and surprised. I quietly responded, "Yes, sir. Thank you, sir."

I was amazed that he chose me. He had only asked me a few questions. I must have provided some really good answers. I hinted a small smirk on my face.

Leonardo looked me straight in the eye, "I remember years ago a boy who showed me that he had the genesis of an artist. That boy has matured and so has his talent." He reciprocated with the faintest hint of a smile. "Now Francesco, before you walk out this door, lose that smile. Be indifferent and unexcited. I do not want the other candidates to know who I have selected."

I nodded to Leonardo in agreement. He continued, "Now, look like you have received displeasure from the Almighty."

As Leonardo unlocked the last bolt and opened the door, I lost all facial expression. I had been hit by the wrath of God. And it felt great.

CHAPTER 4 - THE FIRST DAY

When I got home that evening and told my parents, they were both very, very happy for me. Niccolo and Serena even gave me nice warm hugs. And I was very happy, too. But I felt an odd feeling within me, in the pit of my stomach that moved and turned and twisted. I was nervous. Momma noticed and knew exactly what to do. She made one of my favorite meals to help relieve any uneasiness I had. Mommas are like that, knowing the right thing to do to make you feel better.

As we ate dinner and I shared the day's experiences with them, my anxiety seemed to disappear for the moment. The more I talked about the day, the more comfortable I became. Later, Giovanna came over and congratulated me. She was very proud of my accomplishment. The next day, Giovanna joined us at church. I don't remember that morning as much, except for Giovanna holding my hand throughout the service. We didn't stay long as I had a lot to prepare for the next day, the first day of my new job.

The rest of the day and late into the night, I stayed up writing my thoughts of the interview. I usually jotted down architectural ideas for bridge designs, sketched church layouts, and other miscellaneous ideas that came to my mind. But that evening I wrote what happened during the interview with Leonardo, the layout of his studio, and the opinions and notions he shared with me.

Today also marked the start of a new routine. My journal logs would now be written daily, to record all my experiences, encounters, and lessons from the great Master himself.

In the back of my head I kept thinking: tomorrow was the day, the first day as an apprentice for Leonardo da Vinci. When I turned in for the night and slipped into bed, I knew it was already past midnight. It was now Monday. Needless to say, I did not sleep well, as much as I tried.

My mind chased a myriad of thoughts. I shared a bed with Niccolo and may have disturbed his slumber with my frequent tossing and turning. I landed my first job and I was very excited — and now was very nervous again. I knew I was lucky to even have a job like this, and I did not want to fail as soon as I got started. Sleep. What would be expected of me? How could I make a good impression? What did I need to know on that first day? Sleep.

Was I nervous? Oh, yeah! Was I questioning my skills and architectural abilities? Yes. As an apprentice, starting at the base of Leonardo's mountain of knowledge, was I intimidated at climbing the rugged obstacles placed in front of me, challenging everything I thought I knew? The answer was unequivocally: Yes. Today, I was going to surrender all that I had learned and start fresh. Sleep.

My life was changing and my parents and Giovanna supported me in this transition. Before sunrise and as my new morning wakeup call, Giovanna showed up at my house before the rooster crowed to help put feed in the chicken's troughs. Though I was barely half awake, she provided me the early morning encouragement I needed on my first day.

Momma made my favorite breakfast of pancetta and eggs, a slice of bread, and a cup of tea from a sassafras root. I don't know where Momma or Giovanna got the extra energy at that time in the morning, but I appreciated their lively spirit and smiling faces. I was now energized and ready to start.

On this cloudy day, Giovanna and I left my home and walked briskly through town as I was not going to be late on my first day! We passed over the Ponte Vecchio Bridge, through

the Palazzo della Signoria, and past many businesses that were just opening for the morning. Normally, it was an enjoyable walk where I savored the smells of the bakeries and observed the details and beauty of Florence. Today, my focus was unswerving and direct. Today was business.

Giovanna kept pace with me, hand-in-hand, as we headed to my destination: The Studio. This would be the exciting place to which I traveled each day from here on out.

I arrived at Leonardo's studio in what seemed like minutes, but I know it took a lot longer. I was so distracted for the day ahead that the walk itself was now a blur in my memory. Slightly out of breath, I regained my composure and thanked Giovanna for her kindness and selflessness.

She gave me a kiss on each cheek, and then a big, warm hug. "I'm here for you, whenever you need it." She then surprised me with a kiss on the lips. I always knew Giovanna was special and this morning her love and generosity shined more than ever.

I went upstairs and walked down the darkened, narrow hallway, like I had a couple of days prior. This time, no one was in front of me. No waiting, though I was still nervous.

The floors creaked with every second step I took.

As I reached the main door of the studio, the wood planks transitioned to the alluring circular design. The beautiful symmetry and glow of those lavender flowers warmed my heart and eased my worry. They were a familiar and welcomed friend amid my first-day nervousness.

Before I knocked on the studio door for Leonardo, I heard footsteps behind me. Several footsteps. I turned around and could not see who they were. As they walked down the dark corridor toward me, I saw the silhouettes of three people; the one in front was taller while the two following were shorter. As they got closer, my breathing slowly increased and my heart beat faster. I knew there would be one other apprentice. Who were these three and what did they want? I turned toward the door and knocked quickly three times.

Was I at the wrong place or at the wrong time? Leonardo had said to show up today and to be here at this studio. Was this an unusual initiation? As they approached directly in front of me, the small window accentuated the tall person's shadowed, bearded face.

"Buongiorno, Francesco," exclaimed the one in front. It was Leonardo da Vinci.

"Buongiorno," I replied — and was promptly relieved.

Leonardo turned halfway around, "Meet Cristina and Benvenuto, they will be apprenticing with you." We exchanged greetings and shook each other's hands. I was embarrassed as the palms of my hands were damp and clammy, but more nervous that the new day ahead of me was about to begin.

Leonardo stepped forward in front of the door and reached for the keychain around his neck. Outside, the clouds moved away and the sun shone brightly through the hallway window. I looked to the right and noticed the wooden panels on the wall were different from those around it.

At the same time, Benvenuto placed the palm of his hand on the wall. "Is this a door? There is no handle or latch on it."

Holding two keys firmly in the grip of his hand, Leonardo replied, "This, Benvenuto, is an exit. Only an exit. If you come through that door, then you will have succeeded in leaving."

Cristina and I laughed for a moment. Leonardo was straight-faced and apparently did not think that what he said was amusing. We immediately refrained from giggling and mirrored the same serious face that Leonardo expressed. The hallway turned quiet.

Leonardo raised one key and inserted it into the front door's first lock. He turned the key slowly to the right. I could hear the lock mechanism make one click. The Master inserted the next key into the second lock and proceeded in the same manner as he did with the first key. Leonardo breathed a sigh of relief and confirmation. "Yes."

Not being shy, Cristina asked, "Why are there two keys? Would one lock work just as well?"

"These locks have one function: to stop those who are not welcome." He looked at each of us with a warm, inviting smile, opened the door to the studio, and then held out both hands with a kindhearted greeting. "Here, you are welcome."

As we entered the room, I looked around and gazed with curiosity and wonder. From the interview a couple of days ago, I do not remember seeing anything but a table and chair and the general character of the studio. The center of attention that day was focused directly in front of me: Leonardo da Vinci.

Looking around the room now, there was so much more. To my left, the studio contained several bookcases; two easels; a five foot, three-paneled, movable changing screen that doubled as a sun shade; a shelf for supplies; and a large table with cutting implements. And, I would never forget, a propped-up full body skeleton.

To my right you could see his inventions, sketches, drawings, and writings. There were painted shields and armor that were to be used as altarpieces, along with half-decorated banners, bed frames, *cassoni*[17] chests, and plates.

---

[17] Cassoni → A large wooden chest or container that is ornately gilded, painted, or carved.

Off to one corner, with its door closed, was a small room. Its function, I later discovered, would be one of the most intriguing.

The room's lighting came from the window and a large candelabra with five candles. This helped illuminate our workspace and the walls that were adorned with several paintings of birds, similar to the ones I had seen in the hall-way. There were miniature terracotta frescoed statues, altar tables and rails, *ciboriums*[18] to cover the altar, and tabernacles. All vital to the rituals of the church.

Looking up at the ceiling, there were two round devices, each with three flattened panels connected to its center. A long belt was wrapped around the circumference at its base and ran the length of the room around the second unit. The second unit had another connected belt that ran along the ceiling through the wall. Every few minutes the belts turned and the flattened panels rotated and created a pleasant breeze flowing across our bodies to relieve the torrid summer heat.

Over near Leonardo's desk, there was a sculpture made from a complex of coins and designed in a spiral-like arrangement. I was

---

[18] <u>Ciborium</u> → A large canopy over an altar.

overwhelmed at the considerable virtuosity and finesse with which the Master displayed his talents.

Leonardo closed the door and walked to the center of the room. "Welcome, my apprentices. This studio is organized to provide me with an efficient and productive place to work." He pointed to his left, "Over here, this is where I sculpt. It is where I dream. I design. I mold. I create. It is where you, Cristina, my sculptor apprentice, will learn and provide me with what I need when I need it."

Leonardo walked near the window. "This is where I paint. The light is very special here. It is where I dream. I look. I sketch. I paint. I create. It is where you, Benvenuto, my painter apprentice, will learn and provide me with what I need when I need it."

Leonardo walked further to the right. "This is architecture. It is where I dream. I design. I sketch. I create. It is where you, Francesco, my architect apprentice, will learn and provide me with what I need when I need it."

I looked down at the floor, which was incredibly dusty and dirty. Despite the dirt, the three of us, virgin apprentices in an amazing studio, were in awe. I experienced a feeling of delight and wonder. I saw the same tempered excitement in both Cristina and Benvenuto's eyes that I felt in mine: calm on the outside, heart beating fast on the inside.

Leonardo pulled out three sheets of paper and three quills, and placed them on the desk. "This is a contract for you to work for me as an apprentice. I agree to teach you, provide for your safety, and pay you a small salary. You are working for me and our relationship is collaborative; that is, once you attain the skill level I require of you."

The three of us looked at each of our designated papers on the desk.

"This contract is an agreement between you and me that allows you the perseverance and courage to succeed, the permission to fail and begin again, and the opportunity to discover a new way to triumph. BUT, this contract also restricts you … to not disclose any secrets to anyone outside of this studio."

With my heart beating fast and hand shaking, I thought about my future with Leonardo da Vinci. The extent of knowledge I would acquire from him.

"This time with me will test your patience, enhance your skills, and develop and hone your artistic aptitude. But this apprenticeship will only last one year."

Benvenuto immediately spoke up. "Excuse me, sir. Most apprenticeships last for several years or more."

Leonardo stood up tall and firm. "This apprenticeship is not your ordinary teacher/ student relationship. It will be fast paced and move quickly. This will be a unique system of training you, a new generation of practitioners, for sculpting, painting, and architecture. In addition, each of you will learn a new appreciation for invention, science, music, mathematics, engineering, anatomy, writing, and more, much more." Leonardo turned his body but kept his eyes on us. "If you don't believe you can do this in one year, the door is that way."

This was the best opportunity I would probably ever have and this was a chance I would take. I picked up the pen and signed my contract. Cristina signed her contract. Benvenuto signed his. We placed our pens back on the desk.

"Time will fly and you will grow, and I will have three impressive artists." Leonardo reached for a quill and signed my contract and then the others. He shook each of our hands — slowly, and looking directly into our eyes. I realized that this paper established the foundation for our strong relationship.

He collected all of the contracts. "Follow me." We walked over to a table with an ornately decorated clay urn. "Just because you cannot see something, does not mean it is not there." He picked up a candle and lit the papers we had signed moments earlier. As the flames rose, he tossed the burning papers into the urn. "Material is finite. Paper burns, but the underlying contract between us still exists. The spirit of our contract will forever last as our obligation and responsibility to each other ... for one year."

Leonardo's unusual perspective on life had me marveling at his pragmatic outlook and attitude for every aspect of his being, and his willingness to freely share his thoughts and motivations with others. As the smoke from the papers disappeared, Leonardo placed the lid onto the urn. "Learning never exhausts the mind. I expect you to learn every day. I want you to learn every day. The tools for your success are on you and within you. Use your eyes and other senses to enrich your experience. *Sapere vedere!*[19]"

For our first task of the day, Leonardo taught us how to make paper and prepare quills and ink. His technique for making paper was similar to how Momma taught me several years ago, before Serena was born. She kept a large wicker basket of rags from old clothes and linen. We would go outside and cut up the rags into tiny pieces, and dump them into a vat of boiling water. After about an hour, she rinsed the soggy fabric through a mould[20]. Momma pressed out the liquid using old bricks and then hung the sheets in the sun to dry. Leonardo's approach was similar, but at the end of the process he used long, heavy, and wide wooden planks to squeeze the water out and make the paper more uniform in texture and size.

Not all of his painting surfaces were canvas. Hardboard wooden panels made from poplar

---

[19] *Sapere vedere* → Knowing how to see.
[20] Mould → Also known as a sieve or a filter.

provided a better support than canvas for oils because of the rigid structure that helped prevent cracks in the oil paint. Leonardo showed us step-by-step how to prepare these panels.

This process involved fitting square boards alongside each other with thin layers of glue, stretching linen across the surface, and applying layers of *gesso*[21] paint on top. After each layer of gesso dried, we sanded each coat depending on how rough or smooth Leonardo wanted the surface.

For the pens, Leonardo showed us how to select a good goose feather and shape it into a pointed writing device that would absorb the ink into the quill and draw very fine lines. We made other styluses to round out our complement of tools, each having a different effect: a metal point stylus made of the soft silver metal, and others made out of iron or wood.

Leonardo made his own ink from oak gall, gum arabic, and iron sulphate. With a little practice we were able to mix the ink to the right consistency. We used ink wells that functioned as storage receptacles for the ink.

---

[21] <u>Gesso</u> → A hard compound of chalk, gypsum, or other whiting mixed with glue.

Leonardo was adamant about taking care of all his tools. "You will all be responsible for taking care of all my brushes, pens, and any other implements I use in this studio. Make sure the paint does not dry on the brush. To clean them, soak the brushes in water. I have plenty of rags for you to use. With proper maintenance, these tools will last several months."

He looked straight into our eyes. "Everything I do has a purpose. Every action, a meaning. Knowing is not enough, you must think by observing and listening. Question when you do not understand. And apply what you learn. It is only then that you will comprehend what I am teaching."

My attention was undivided. My mind was open and ready to absorb what was needed.

"You will help me. And I will show you, train you, and teach you. One can have no smaller or greater mastery than mastery of oneself."

I only hoped that I could meet what was expected of me.

CHAPTER 5 - TRAINING AND LEARNING

Over the next month, Cristina, Benvenuto, and I showed up each day to work and learn techniques and style in Leonardo's studio. The more we worked together, the more we learned about each other.

Cristina Novella Rosso lived in a small house within walking distance from the *Cattedrale di Santa Maria del Fiore*[22], a Roman Catholic church at the center of Florence where she was also baptized.

She was fourteen years old, the same age I was. Cristina had beautiful long dark hair with a rich chestnut color. My initial drawings could not deliver justice to her enchanted beauty. In the studio, she bundled her hair up in a headdress or tied it back so it would not get in

---

[22] Cattedrale di Santa Maria del Fiore → Also known as the Cathedral of Saint Mary of the Flowers.

the way of her work. She was a perfectionist and didn't want anything to stop her from achieving her goal.

Cristina was an only child and lived alone with her mother, Piera. Her father died from an illness when she was five years old. The clergy and parish were a tremendous help for Piera and Cristina during their time of grieving. To further the healing process, a young priest introduced them to a variety of activities at the church, including music and art. This is where Cristina learned to express herself vocally and with her hands. Soft moldable clay became her love. Cristina enjoyed the feel of the cool, wet clay in her hands and how easy it was to form into other shapes. She learned and became a natural at the potter's wheel, working daily in the church basement producing plates, cups, and vases. She brought into our studio several of her finished works that had been glazed with beautiful designs.

Cristina's interests progressed with her fascination in sculpting. To her, clay was magical; she could transform a block of cold, lifeless clay into the most beautiful living shapes. Cristina's passion helped support her mother with additional income to pay for their living expenses. When Cristina heard about the opportunity to learn from Leonardo da Vinci, she was eager and excited to rise to a higher level. Cristina shared with me, "I have a special gift given to me by God. This is the studio where I will nurture my talents for a greater good." Cristina planned on opening her own business in town with the hope of sharing her art and passion with others.

Benvenuto Domenico Farnese, whom we nicknamed Ben, came from the town of Empoli, southwest of Florence. Before he moved to Florence for this apprenticeship, Ben lived on his father's farm, where he grew a variety of grain and vegetables.

He was a little older than I was, a bit more than fifteen years old. He was the oldest of five children, all of them boys. Ben's father never remarried after his mother died giving birth to their fifth child. Ben's role in the family was to help his father on the farm and to help raise the younger boys.

The first time I saw Ben was on our first day at the studio. I noticed his eyes, dark brown and mysterious, shared with strong arched brows and thick eyelashes, and a nonchalant gaze and no perceptible smile — he seemed so serious.

He wore a neatly stitched linen doublet[23] that gathered closely at his neck and wrists. His momma had probably been like mine and told him to make a good impression on his first day at work.

In contrast to Ben's neatly kept, tousled, brown hair, mine was longer. Since Giovanna enjoyed running her hand through my hair, I kept up with its daily grooming. One of these days, I'll change my style just to freshen things up and surprise Giovanna and maybe even Momma.

That first day, we were both equally nervous. The more we talked, the more we both opened up to each other. He became one of my best friends.

---

[23] <u>Doublet</u> → A man's short close-fitting padded jacket.

Ben started painting when he was five. During rain storms he would go outside and use the mud from around the house and draw all sorts of images on the side of the house and barn, and sometimes right on the animals. He even ventured to create masterpieces on his neighbors' houses. Of course, his father did not approve of these particular canvases and had him wash away his work as soon as the neighbors complained. In response to these complaints, his father created a small area of wall along the inside of the barn where he resumed his artistic talents using charcoal from the wood stove.

Ben's drawings started with stick figures of people and animals and evolved into more discernible and appealing images. When he was nine, Ben became friends with two local artists in town and obtained extra pieces of scrap paper from them. The artists helped teach him the finer techniques of sketching, drawing, and painting. This was when Ben's drawing talents and skills matured. He would spend a full day walking around town, going from one artist to the next, picking up supplies, and listening and learning from them. Something in Ben had clicked and his aspirations to become a painter were firmly set. Ben told me that his acceptance into Leonardo's studio would help pay for much-needed repairs on his family's farm. Leonardo provided Ben a place to stay in an extra room in his house. This helped Ben save even more money for his family. Ben planned to return home often to lend his father and brothers a hand.

As Leonardo focused his attention and energy on a specific artistic discipline, Cristina, Ben, and I watched closely and assisted him in his tasks. "Before you can create, you need to understand the basics and primitives." Leonardo showed us the proper way to hold a brush. He handed us each a brush. "First, you hold the brush like you are passing a pen to someone. With a loose grip, apply pressure with your thumb holding the body of the brush against your index and middle finger."

Ben and Cristina's technique was perfect. They each had years of experience learning from other artists. My approach was not as mature. Leonardo worked with me to get my technique right, holding my hands and shaping the contours of my fingers. He was pleasant, calm, and patient as I adapted and learned his way.

Leonardo showed us other styles of brushes and different ways of holding each. "When the brush is held near the end of the handle, the brushstrokes become looser, lighter, and paint is applied less carefully. The farther away your fingertips are from the bristles, the lighter the brushstroke." He showed us how to paint fine detail and even provided us with a *mahl stick*[24] to help steady our hand when painting fine details. Leonardo enjoyed teaching us by example. Somehow, he was more engaged when sharing his knowledge and experience.

After he completed one painting, he challenged us to replicate what he had done using the same style, same technique, same everything. "The heavens and the earth were created in seven days. Every aspect of painting requires you to think before you do. Take one step at a time; art is progressive. Remember what you saw me do, my approach, my brush strokes, my focus and patience."

---

[24] Mahl stick → A lightweight stick used by artists to support the working hand to avoid touching a vertical working surface.

With three easels surrounding Leonardo's seat, we worked on our paintings; we reviewed his drawing and focused on our re-creations.

When we completed our task, Leonardo reviewed each drawing closely. He stood back and crossed his arms in deep thought.

I glanced at Cristina and Ben's drawings and noticed they were both very similar to mine. Unfortunately, none of them was quite like Leonardo's.

Leonardo walked toward the middle of the studio. "Come over here. Circle around me." We surrounded him and waited.

"Just like God created his masterpiece, art follows a similar creation with seven basic yet essential principles. Close your eyes. Imagine you are holding a painting palette and brush to draw a bird. It is early morning near a beautiful lake. Think carefully where you want to place the bird on the canvas and how far away to draw the mountains and sky. There is a light mist above the lake where the bird is flying, so reflect that movement with the mist. The night stars are slowly fading away to the rising golden sun, but the moon is still brilliantly displayed with its intricate features. Now open your eyes."

I opened my eyes and smiled at Leonardo. Cristina and Ben shared grins with each other. I imagined every step and every brush stroke in my mind. I wasn't a skilled painter, but my imagination didn't know that. My creation was still vivid in my mind, with a purple heron flying over the lake just at sunrise.

Leonardo explained, "You have just created art and applied the principles of proportion, movement, variety, emphasis, rhythm, balance, and harmony. Now, art is not complete until it has this. There is an eighth concept that will push your work into a masterpiece."

Leonardo looked around the room to see if we knew that last concept. Cristina and Ben shook their heads. Leonardo looked at me and grinned. "Francesco?"

I responded, "I have heard that if you create from your heart, then you give your creation a soul and spirit."

"Correct. Very good. Your heart composes those separate, lifeless objects into a unifying overall image. The picture you created in your mind of the bird and mist and sunrise now give life to the painting. The singing bird enchants your ears, the cool mist flows across your body, and the sun warms your face. That is the essence we all must strive to create."

I continued my day with Leonardo, sketching and drafting architectural designs with him. He asked Cristina and Ben to join us while we worked. He believed that the world and our capabilities were not destined for only one artistic discipline, but that the expression or application of human creative skill and imagination was multifaceted. There was crossover and integration in the arts, and this marriage would be powerful, beautiful, and emotionally fulfilling.

I learned painting and sculpting techniques and styles that could be directly applied to my architecture. The methodical and systematic approach for products we created appeared sophisticated, yet was simple in nature.

We learned about color and how different shades accented shadows. Leonardo showed us murals that used Pompeiian red, a rich red ochre color that had an ample amount of pigment made from iron oxide. Specific colors were to be used sparingly and specifically, in order to call attention to features. Blending and mixing a palette of bold or even monotone colors allowed for a larger amalgam of possibilities in our creative artistic spectrum — defining shadows, emphasizing perspectives, and presenting divergent orientations.

Later in our training, Leonardo laid the foundation and design for one of his projects. We were instructed how to finish the piece. The painting. The sketch. The sculpture. He showed us every aspect of what he had laid out and what was needed to finish. However, this did not happen immediately and was different for each of us. It was only once we showed proficiency and mastery of techniques and skill, and a comprehensive understanding of what he expected, that this would take place.

Throughout our training, we provided Leonardo with our undivided attention. Ben and I absorbed everything he said. Cristina, without fail, wrote down her notes during and after every session. I did not know how she could keep up with all the information Leonardo shared with us. I needed a hands-on learning approach to help me embed those ideas and practices into my daily routine.

With all artistic ventures, there were joys of working on a project as well as the by-products of those joys. As apprentices, we were also instructed to perform menial tasks. We cleaned painting palettes and brushes, changed the chamber pot, prepared blank canvases, sharpened charcoal pencils, changed the chamber pot, prepared lime plaster, mixed pigments in a mortar and pestle, cleaned trowels and scrapers, and changed the chamber pot — again.

Yet even these necessary chores often provided unexpected opportunities for learning and creative discovery. For example, with regard to the chamber pot, I could ascertain what certain people ate the night before or earlier in the day. And then describe the wonderful palette of colors and hues and textures in which to recreate, if desired, the object in its original magnificence, but in a more pleasing state. On certain slow days, these creative thought processes helped me pass the time.

Whether exercising our musings, artistic talents, or other tasks assigned that day, we always worked quietly. We did not want to disrupt Leonardo's concentration. Several hours each day, he gazed out the window or walked circles around the studio — all while seemingly not accomplishing anything.

Almost every day, though, Leonardo retreated into the secretive backroom of the studio, for hours on end, without a word and without interruption. That was the one area of the studio that was expressly forbidden for us to enter. When he was done, he left that room just as silently. Cristina, Ben, and I would glance at each other and whisper to each other, trying to guess what might have happened.

I had my own suspicions about the purpose of Leonardo's secret chamber. I believed that all artists or inventors or engineers, or anyone with a creative mind, had to sift through their ideas, organize them, shuffle them around, and critique them from all sides and from all aspects. For that, he needed a quiet place of solitude for uninterrupted, focused thought, reflection, and concentration — whatever was needed.

My own home offered no isolation since my brother and sister persistently disturbed my train of thought. I could appreciate Leonardo wanting to get away from any distractions. But for hours at a time? I suspected he may either be in deep thought — or deep sleep.

At the beginning of each morning, before we began our work, Leonardo had us proclaim that each day would be a success. With a collective gusto and smile, we enthusiastically announced, *"Agite Excelsius!*[25]*"* This daily phrase set the tempo for our work. All our learning, creative activities, and discussions would be guided by this open frame of mind. A positive attitude and a healthy outlook were important to our overall success. At the end of the day before we left the studio, Leonardo had us gather and all proudly state, *"Agite Excelsius!"*

---

[25] *Agite Excelsius* → Latin for "Go to a place higher up, accomplish even greater things."

CHAPTER 6 - SHADOW DANCING

One afternoon when the day was uncomfortably hot and humid, and the air was oppressively stagnant, Leonardo took a longer than usual nap during *riposo*[26]. With his head firmly resting on top of the desk, Leonardo lay motionless for at least an hour, breathing heavily with customary snorts every few minutes to break up the monotony. Even a few *fare un peto*[27] were heard from his desk, echoing against the wooden chair. If it wasn't for the rotation of the fans above us, circulating and dissipating the newly created air, we would have certainly fainted from the aroma.

During our break, Cristina, Ben, and I relaxed and ate our lunch in the back of the studio. Cristina ate her lunch slowly and

---

[26] <u>Riposo</u> → Also known as a siesta. This traditional early afternoon shutdown usually lasts about 90 minutes to two hours.

[27] <u>Fare un peto</u> → Passing gas.

carefully coddled her left wrist. She had worked on a clay sculpture earlier in the morning and injured it. Usually she warmed up her muscles before starting and took regular breaks throughout the day, stretching and changing up her patterns — careful not to force her muscles to stay in the same position for a long time. This morning, she went longer without taking a break and suffered the consequences. Her wrist would most likely be fine tomorrow.

Other days while eating lunch, we would wander around the studio inspecting several of Leonardo's inventions more closely.

Today we noticed a leather-bound manuscript made up of folio sheets resting on the corner of his desk. We discussed among ourselves what secrets were contained within. Were they notes or drawings for future inventions? Scientific or mechanical illustrations? Our curiosity increased with every passing moment.

After much whispered debate, Cristina decided to find out. She stood up and approached the desk, stepping gingerly across the wooden and sometimes creaking floor.

With her thumb and forefinger, she delicately lifted up the book.

Both Ben's and my hearts were beating fast, yet we were holding our breaths in restrained anticipation.

As Cristina leaned forward to remove the manuscript, the floor decided to protest vehemently: CREAK!

Leonardo raised his head and grabbed Cristina's hand, stopping her immediately. We all froze. We were dead. Caught red-handed, two accomplices watching the perpetrator in the act of this unfathomable crime of curiosity.

A bit groggy from his rest, Leonardo proclaimed, "Everyone and everything has a purpose. Beauty interacts with life in ways we cannot comprehend. When it follows its true nature, when it is in balance with its environment, its soul can shine brightly. Light and shadows and objects and ... books."

Cristina gently released the book as Leonardo took hold of it.

Leonardo continued, "It may not make sense how you should perceive the world around you. So you must change your perspective. Free your mind from all obstacles. It is then, and only then, that you will release your imagination and see divine providence in all things."

Leonardo finished, "Order is the precise and harmonious arrangement of things. To restore order from disorder, we must see its function as intended by the Creator." Carefully, he placed the book back on the desk, with meticulous attention to the original position and orientation where it once rested.

Leonardo picked up a mirror and moved toward the window. He placed the mirror on the window ledge, redirecting a beam of light toward the book. He asked Cristina to join him at his desk. Still startled from before, she obliged and joined him. Leonardo positioned her next to him and pointed his hand forward.

It was in this position that the beam of light reflected by the mirror created a new image on the wall. This image, created from a series of independent objects in the path of the light, formed shadow art. Art created by the absence of light. The new image on the wall was that of a gondola floating down a canal in Venezia[28]. The rise of heat from the mirror's surface created a silhouetted flow of moving water for the boat.

---

[28] Venezia → Venice.

Leonardo pointed to a series of individual objects that were in line with the path of the light. "It is a matter of perspective. A place for everything and everything in its place."

Cristina smiled and responded, "It is beautiful. The way that light and shadows play together. It is absolutely beautiful."

Leonardo smiled at his unique artistic achievement. He picked up the book and asked Cristina to put it away on the bookshelf. As she followed his instruction, Leonardo redirected the mirror into another direction.

After a brief yawn, he spoke up, "I am feeling generous this very hot day. Let's say we stop and head out. Everyone, please clean up your stations."

As it had been warmer than normal, we had not worked as much in the morning. Ben and Cristina quickly cleaned up the paint brushes and rags and stood by the door. I swept the floor, which was dustier than normal. Leonardo, seeing that Ben and Cristina were ready to leave, walked to the door and unlocked it.

I looked up at the three of them standing at the door. I stopped what I was doing and, in four part harmony, we announced, *Agite*

Excelsius! I still had some sweeping to do so I went back to my task. Benvenuto and Cristina left.

As I finished up, Leonardo expressed satisfaction with my work, "Francesco, I have been watching you and see great potential in your work."

I thanked him with a nod as I swept the dusty and grubby floor.

Leonardo continued, "But to become great you must tap your inner genius ... rethink how you approach your work."

I collected the debris into a dustpan and asked the Master, "I see ideas in my mind that are crystal clear. And I put them on paper. But something gets lost in the process and I end up throwing it away."

Leonardo explained, "You don't take a hot bath by stepping directly into the scalding water. You test it with your finger, then toes. You pour cold water as needed then test again with your finger. Then your foot, and then your whole body. You move slowly so that you don't burn yourself." I finished cleaning and turned to heed his advice.

He continued, "Call it process, or methodology, or approach. It is all organized thought. If you find you're not tapping into your genius, rethink how you approach your work. The world needs your talents, Francesco. Can you imagine our lives without the benefit of your ideas? The key is discovering what works for you." Leonardo went over to the bookshelf and filed some scrolls.

I stood up, walked toward the window, and moved the folding screen aside. At early afternoon, the sun was beaming into the room. As I was about to pick up the mirror and close the shutters, I noticed the beam of light from the mirror going a different direction than before. Straight through the coin structure on a pedestal near Leonardo's desk. A new image had appeared: Atlas[29] holding celestial spheres on his shoulders.

I stopped for a few moments and admired the image with amazement and delight.

Leonardo walked up to my side. "Time is yet another object of the Divine that can be used as a companion with our lives." Leonardo moved the mirror and closed the shutters. The Atlas image dissolved as magically as it arrived.

---

[29] Atlas → In Greek mythology, Atlas was a legendary Titan.

I picked up some supplies to take home and work with later. Leonardo walked out the door and asked me to close the door when I left.

With Leonardo fifteen paces in front of me, I walked through the doorway slowly. Today with a close eye, I inspected the locking mechanisms that were built into the door and doorframe. Ever since I started as his apprentice, those door locks had always intrigued me. I am an engineer, after all! How did the self-locking mechanism work?

I noticed a cable integrated into the door, at waist height, that traversed between the inside edge of the door and the frame. Almost hidden from view, I wondered about its function. I determined that it was most likely a spring apparatus that helped engage the lock. Whatever it was, its contribution to the larger locking function was a work of art. As I closed the door, locks clicked shut and in that moment, I was captivated at such an elegant device.

Leonardo called out, "Come now."

I acknowledged him and proceeded down the hallway. I took my time as I walked. Looking around me, I was enchanted and mesmerized at the beauty which Leonardo had given life. From the symmetrical complexity and beauty of the floor design to the masterpiece frescoes and sketches on the walls, Leonardo's creations epitomized his soul and spirit. We exited the building and headed our different directions.

The day's heat and humidity were still heavy in the air. With every step I took, sweat bounced off my brow, trickled down my cheek and neck, and soaked my shirt. This was a normal Florence summer day, though today my gait was light and vibrant.

It was studio sessions like this that I looked forward to, where Leonardo unsuspectingly surprised us and triggered our curiosity. We were his children anxious to learn something new and avant-garde. Today's lesson opened our eyes and had us see and experience objects from a fresh and different perspective: to see beyond what was normal and explore new dimensions. Today was an enlightened day.

CHAPTER 7 - THE SQUABBLE

Several days later at the studio, during mid-morning, Leonardo stepped out for a break. The three of us continued working on our project designs. Cristina was fine-tuning sketches of a sculpture for a local may-or. Ben was fin-ishing a rough drawing and shadings of the *Torre di Pisa*[30]. I was drafting

---

[30] <u>Torre di Pisa</u> → Italian for "Tower of Pisa," a campanile or freestanding bell tower.

preliminary architectural designs for an extension to a monastery at the edge of town.

Leonardo taught us the importance of framing our vision around what we wanted to create. When drawing, he mentioned that charcoal was an excellent medium to use at the beginning as it was flexible to express details. And, in its versatility, charcoal could be used to produce either a soft or strong quality of line, which could be erased without difficulty, or it could be dragged across the paper to produce different tonal areas, texture, and shading. I enjoyed this part of the architectural process. These drawing and design techniques help shape the idea in my head into a solid artistic vision.

As the morning continued, the wind outside picked up and it started to rain. Ben was nearest to the window and went over and closed the shutters. Walking back, he looked over at my drawings and then to Cristina's sketches. "Hmm," he groaned.

Cristina quickly responded in a challenging tone, "What does that mean, Ben? Something wrong with our work? Not good enough for you?"

Ben turned around and faced Cristina with an indifferent and unexcited expression. "The greatest art is painting. Sculpture is nice, but lacks color and beauty."

Cristina peered over at Ben and looked at him in confusion.

Ben continued in a condescending tone, "Painting has greater potential for expression, to render colors and texture to create an illusion of anything."

I crossed my arms and listened intently. Was this a battle of the arts?

Cristina looked very much annoyed and responded in a passionate and confident demeanor, "That is a very interesting observation, Ben. But what you don't see is that sculpture is more worthy and resilient than a painting because it is not afraid of fire or heat or cold. It is ... eternal. The beauty of the human body is exposed in many dimensions through sculpture; not only can you see muscles and body contours, but you can feel how they all connect together."

I leaned back in my chair and looked at Ben, "She does have a point, Ben."

Cristina turned to me and announced emphatically, "Now, what I don't understand is, why you are here in this studio? What is 'architecture'? It is a simple craft and noble profession, but very different from … art."

I couldn't believe what I heard. Did she just attack me? I was seeing a totally different side to both of them. I was ready to enter this intellectual brawl and defend my profession and integrity. I stood up slowly and confidently replied to the accusations, "Architecture is the basis for everything that is built. Everything. Bridges, buildings … to where we work and live. This very building and studio came from architecture. It is a form of art. Sometimes the art is massive. It has texture, color, depth, and ultimately, function. It has beauty from many perspectives." There, I said it. My heart was beating much faster now than thirty-seconds ago.

Unaffected by this mindless banter, Ben stepped back into the fray, "Yes, yes. That is all good. Settle down, both of you." He looked at me and smiled in an unconcerned way. "Painting requires more mental ability than physical effort. There is unique technical skill that elevates this art to the level of a scholarly endeavor. Painting portrays the three-dimensional qualities of sculpture."

Cristina stepped toward Ben with an anger in her eyes I had not seen before.

Ben looked at me and continued, "Now for architecture, I can't take a building with me and show it to my colleagues or my mother. I could sketch or paint your building. That would be much easier to show. Not all that rock and plaster to deal with."

Cristina picked up several charcoal fragments and hurled them at Ben, striking one large piece square on his left cheek. "Stop saying that. That's mean!"

Ben grabbed a bundle of brushes in each hand and flung them toward Cristina and me. Both of us ducked and avoided getting hit. "No, that's mean."

It was either get hit or hit back. I looked around and crumpled several sheets of paper into small round projectile balls and threw them at Ben.

Cristina yelled, "Both of you, stop it!" as she threw clay wads at both Ben and me.

Tempers were on the rise and the intensity in our voices reflected that. Our artistic discourse was a passionate defense for what we loved. We were protecting our inner soul. I didn't dislike paintings or sculptures. We were all artists. Different types of artists. Art was an expression of human creative skill and imagination producing works to be appreciated for their beauty or emotional power.

I took cover behind my area and breathed deeply, waiting for my heart to return to a normal beat. I looked over at Cristina and with a calm, collected demeanor offered, "Okay. Okay. Stop." Looking around the room at each of them, I tried to neutralize the situation. "We all love our art. I would design and build an art museum with tall marble Corinthian columns and elaborate capitals decorated with acanthus leaves and scrolls. Inside I would design galleries to exhibit all your beautiful sculptures, Cristina." Directing my attention to Ben, "And between those galleries, I would design long halls with ornate features and tall ceilings to exhibit your magnificent paintings and frescoes, Ben."

There it was, a welcome and possibly uneasy silence in the studio. Did I resolve our artistic differences and settle this expressive dispute? Cristina and Ben looked at the floor and around the room with empathy. I could hear rain starting to hit against the shutters instead of our negative and myopic repartee striking against our pride.

As I looked at them, our pause in discourse was replaced by an unpleasant sound: a *fare un peto* that emanated from the studio door, along with the usual smell that came with it. Leonardo was standing at the threshold. I'm not sure for how long, but probably long enough. The silence this time was deafening. All of us turned to face Leonardo, with our heads and hearts weighed with guilt. We had disgraced all that he was passionate about and had been disrespectful with each other.

In a monotone voice, Leonardo submitted, "It is raining outside and I see there was a storm in here. So, that is enough work for today. My apprentices need time to dry off." The sudden sound of thunder outside reverberated through our motionless bodies. The rain picked up in intensity.

Leonardo continued, "The head and heart and feet are separate, but connected to one body. Each is a different part of the anatomy having a specific function. Without one, the others struggle. Working together, they flourish." He paused and looked at each of us directly. His voice raised in anger, "This is my studio, not your battlefield! An artist must always be respected. Each art is a blend of many disciplines and does not stand by itself."

Leonardo stepped aside and presented the studio exit door. "Your words and actions define who you are and the world you want to live in. My question to you is: Who are you? Now, clean up this mess and leave. Come back tomorrow and show me who you really are."

Today, there was no *Agite Excelsius*. It was a shortened day and not for pleasant reasons. We quickly picked up the debris and left the studio. None of us looked each other in the eye. We were wrong and acted childish, but that was to be addressed another day.

That late morning's storms were like none I had experienced before. The first squall stemmed from the debate and dispute among Cristina, Ben, and me. We were acting like misbehaved children. Our fundamental misunderstanding and singular focus within our artistic disciplines drove us to ignore the inherent beauty and similar expressive qualities of the other arts. In the heat of battle, it was easy for me to forget the aesthetic pleasure each art form had to offer to its audience.

The second storm, a torrential downpour outside during our squabble and early walk home, helped me realize the power of nature, not only for its strength through wind and rain, but to appreciate the other aspects that provided a positive outcome to its audience — our community. The rain enhances the fertility of soil, which sustains the seeds in the field, and nourishes the crops, which brings a plentiful harvest. Everything is connected and works together peacefully.

The long walk home and self-reflection reinforced my understanding of what art means to the artist — which is very personal and expresses their inner soul. The artist's spirit provides the energy, artistic emotion, and balance to create their magnum opus. By the time I reached home, my understanding and appreciation for the artist was much clearer.

CHAPTER 8 - THE TRIP

I woke up at dawn like other mornings and fed the chickens. I dressed and left home for the studio. I walked the same path as I always did, but this time, the walk seemed longer than normal. I found myself walking up and down the same streets, sometimes going around the same block. My mind was thinking about what happened yesterday. Working in the same room as Cristina and Ben would be awkward, but facing Leonardo would be a more difficult challenge. When I arrived at the front steps outside the studio, I paused before going in. I was still feeling anxious and nervous.

I composed myself and took several deep breaths. As I advanced forward, I heard the sound of horses in the back of the building. I proceeded to the rear and saw several oxen- and horse-drawn carriages with boxed crates and cloaked objects loaded into their beds.

Several men unloaded the items and carried them into the building. Some crates were hoisted up by rope on the outside of the building.

Watching ten paces away from me were Cristina and Ben. By the looks of things, they had already made up and weren't harboring any ill feelings to each other. They looked over at me for a quick moment and then turned their focus to the activity in front of us. We stayed there for several minutes until the last of the items was removed from the wagons.

With increasing interest as to the contents of those boxes, the three of us proceeded swiftly into the building and upstairs toward the studio. All of us kept quiet as we walked, only allowing the squeaks in the floor to penetrate the uneasy silence. I kept my pace slow enough so I was at least two meters behind them. I wasn't ready to apologize right then, though my heart was ready to.

As we entered the hallway, the last two burly crew members were exiting the studio. Leonardo was at the doorway. "*Grazie*[31], Lorè, Alessandro."

---

[31] <u>Grazie</u> → Thank you.

Both men replied in their gruff but pleasant voices, "*Prego*[32]."

We had to squeeze our thin bodies against the wall to make enough room for the two workers to pass. Leonardo entered the doorway as we approached. Peering inside the studio, I saw several large crates loaded two-high along with the large objects, still under cloak.

Ben innocently and mournfully asked, "We are here to work, sir. What are in these containers? Are they supplies? Do we need to unpack them today?"

Leonardo swung the studio door toward us and spoke up, "I need to leave town for a meeting in Milan with Ludovico Sforza. The Duke has requested we meet to discuss a project of his. I will be there for about one week."

The door closed and the locks engaged with their familiar sound. He continued, "The boxes do not need to be unpacked. They are a work-in-progress for special customers and I need them to be protected here in the studio while I am away."

---

[32] <u>Prego</u> → You are welcome.

Cristina kindly offered, "We will watch them and make sure no one comes into the studio."

Leonardo looked at each of us and without any facial reaction, "No! That is okay. While I am gone, do not show up at the studio. Continue your work at home and study the material I've provided you. The studio remains locked until I get back."

His voice was firm and he was not negotiating. This was a sudden and unexpected change in schedule. Aside from yesterday's altercation, he could trust us.

Ben asked him, "I don't have an easel at home and I need my paints. If I could…"

Leonardo swiftly interrupted in a coarse tone, "… No one is permitted in the studio. These works are very important and they are not ready to be revealed." Then with a short pause and a calmer, gentler voice, "You may continue your sketches at home. Next week, I will be back and you may continue your work in studio."

We had to wait. Period. There was no questioning him any further.

"One week!"

I couldn't tell if Leonardo's sudden change was warranted because of the nature of the covered items or if it was a result of his apprentices' antics the day before. Leonardo proceeded down the hall and left the building.

The three of us followed him and went our ways. Repairing our relationships with Leonardo and each other would have to happen another day.

CHAPTER 9 - EXPOSING SECRETS

Throughout the rest of the day and into the night, I couldn't help thinking about the studio. What secret was Leonardo keeping from us? Why was he so protective? What "art" must be kept under covers?

During the night, another rainstorm ensued. The consistent patter of raindrops on the shingles should have been hypnotic and pulled me to sleep. But my mind was active and occupied with curiosity. I gazed at the ceiling while Niccolo slept.

Due to their sensitive content, Leonardo's boxes and cloaked objects were held *sub rosa*[33]. Were they unfinished paintings or sculptures of a dignitary? Or, special architectural drawings for a new cathedral? Were they uncompleted pieces of music that would be performed for the Pope? Or, were they mechanical designs or

---

[33] *Sub rosa* → Happening or done in secret.

inventions that would change the course of military battle? Why so secretive that he would not allow us, his apprentices and close confidants, to see?

I had to know what was stored in the studio and I had one week to find out. The sooner the better. Getting in would be simple. What could be the harm? I could keep those secrets held close and Leonardo would never know.

In the morning, while I did errands into town, I met up with Giovanna.

She gave me a warm, long hug and asked me, "Why have you been so busy? Your work can't be that important."

I gave her a kiss, hoping that that she would forgive me. I told her, "I am sorry. Being an apprentice keeps me busy during the day, and when I return home, I am very tired."

As we walked around town and through the market, I thought about how much I enjoyed being with Giovanna. I wanted to spend more time together. I mentioned to her, "This Sunday after church, they are having dancing and singing. Let's stay. It will be fun."

She agreed and gave me a big kiss on the lips, which put a smile on my face. We walked back to her home and I told her that Leonardo went out of town and that I would be working at home.

She stopped and asked me face to face, "If he is away, can you show me the studio?"

I figured I could easily unlock the door and show her around. Plus, I could take a quick peek at some of the hidden, secret items in the studio. With strong desire to relieve my curiosity, I responded on a positive note, "Yes, we can go. Let's head there later tonight." She smiled again, but more brightly, and gave me another kiss. I must have been doing something right.

With Leonardo's studio, I knew what I was doing. Everything would be fine and no one would find out.

CHAPTER 10 - FROM PLAN INTO ACTION

After eating dinner with my family, I went into my bedroom and reached under my bed for my collector's box. This was a small wooden box with intricate designs on its sides that I received as a gift from my parents when I was young. I kept various small toys and other items within it; specifically, my collection of keys.

I had a fascination with keys partly because of their unique and interesting shapes. And because their fundamental design was literally the key to unlocking that which someone wants protected. For a five-year-old, the keys were magical. Though I didn't understand locks, it seemed like the differences between keys were small.

My collection was obtained over several years from our family friend, Giorgio, who was a locksmith. The keys were used and worn, and were from locks that were either damaged beyond repair or lost altogether. Giorgio collected the keys and offered them to me in exchange for helping him at his shop. My collection numbered around fifty. They were from old doors and cabinets, to locks of all sizes.

I threaded the keys through some thin rope and put them over my head. If I was going to gain access to the studio, I needed to get past the two locks that Leonardo had put in place. The more keys I took with me, the more I had a chance of opening the locks.

With an oil lantern in hand and a necklace full of keys, I headed into town. The full moon shone brightly onto the muddy road and puddles. I stopped at Giovanna's house and waited for her to come out. Dressed for a casual walk into town, she carried an oil lantern like mine, only smaller. We walked hand-in-hand to the studio. A few cats and rats scurried in the shadows.

As we approached a couple of blocks from the studio, the silhouettes of two people turned the corner, heading away from us. We quickly escaped notice down a narrow walkway between two buildings and waited for several minutes. We were on a secret mission and wanted it to remain that way.

When the coast was clear, Giovanna and I entered Leonardo's studio building and walked up the stairs. The only light was that from our lanterns. I could feel the grip of her hand get tighter as we walked down the long, dark hallway. A casual and pleasant walk during the day had transformed into a strange and mysterious stroll at night. The wooden floor creaked as we walked slowly down the hall. Our footsteps echoed against the hallway walls and contributed to my nervousness and now sweaty palms.

Our lanterns swayed back and forth, creating eerie moving shadows. The wall's stunning fresco bird drawings turned into unrestrained skeletons roaming their burial crypt. Larger than life. My imagination was taking me down a dark alley. With Giovanna's hand also feeling clammy, I could only wonder where Giovanna's thoughts were. I offered her comfort, "The studio is right there at the end of the hall."

Holding the lantern in front of me, it lit up the walls and floor as we walked. The wooden

Brad Jefferson

planks changed into the beautiful, lavender iris drawing overlaid onto the alluring spiral design. We stopped in front of the door and got ready for the next phase.

I told Giovanna, "I must take you to the studio during the day. The drawings on these walls are impressive. The inlay of wood and display of color of this spiral creation below our feet is spectacular."

Giovanna responded in a monotone, non-excited voice, "Ah ha." I guess she was into a different type of art.

As we stopped at the studio door, Giovanna gave a sigh of relief and let go my hand. I wiped my moist hands onto my shirt and pulled out the bundle of keys from around my neck.

"This won't take long. One of these keys will work and we'll be in the studio in no time."

"Why doesn't Leonardo give you a key? Wouldn't that make it easier?"

I thought to myself how Leonardo might have trusted his apprentices if they hadn't misbehaved like squabbling kids. I replied and lied to Giovanna, "He went out of town and didn't have an extra key. He was going to have one made when he got back." That seemed to satisfy her questions.

Placing the lantern closer to the lock, I inspected the locks' openings and shapes to determine their potential key size. I ruffled through the keys until I found two I thought would work. Probably the first of many keys I would try that night.

I tested each key, slowly inserting them into the lock. After what seemed like several hours, working two-thirds through the keychain, I wondered if I knew what I was doing.

Giovanna was getting impatient. "You said this was going to work. I'm getting tired. Let's leave and come back during the day."

Having gone all this way, I didn't want to give up. Not yet. "Please, Giovanna. A few more keys, please." I sped up testing the keys, but it wasn't pleasing Giovanna.

"I'm going home. We can see the studio in the daylight when Leonardo gets back."

I knew this was the best time for me to see the secrets in Leonardo's studio. Tonight was the night.

Giovanna turned around and started walking away. "Good night, Francesco. I'll be fine walking back. See you tomorrow."

Still focused on my task and fumbling with the keys, I replied, "Sorry it's so late. I'm going to finish with these keys and catch up to you."

"Good night, Francesco." Giovanna headed back down the hallway.

As her lantern faded, I turned around and continued with the remaining keys. I was getting weary-eyed too and was close to calling it quits.

I pulled out the next two keys and inserted the first key into the lock. It fit. Then the second key went into the next lock. Also a perfect fit. I turned the first key slowly to the right. I heard a click in the lock mechanism. "Yes," I murmured to myself. I turned the second key slowly to the right, but it only turned part of the way. I forced the key further. Still no click. No sound at all. It must be really close.

Behind me, down the hall, I heard a sound. A creak from the wooden floor. I turned and saw a shadow. "Giovanna? You came back. I think I got it."

There was no answer. The shadow moved toward me, making creaks with every step it took. The steps and its pace increased. I looked back again and called out. "Gio!?" The shadow was larger and wider than Giovanna. That wasn't Giovanna. I wasn't supposed to be here. If I could only get this door opened — now!

I turned and eyed the door with a sense of urgency. Was the door's position restricting the locked bolt from moving? I grasped the doorknob and pulled it toward me. Nothing. One more time, I pulled and then gave it a forceful shove forward as hard as I could.

At that instant, which probably lasted only a fraction of a second, I heard a low rumbling directly beneath my feet coming from the floor below. The squealing sound of gears grabbed my attention further. The shadow was certainly closer to me, but something else was happening.

I looked down and saw the floor open up. Five beautiful, iris-decorated panels opened their mouth to devour their prey. Before I could jump out of the way, the resulting chasm swiftly swallowed its catch. Me!

CHAPTER 11 - INTO THE DARKNESS

I fell through the floor, a trap door. Holding the lantern protectively in one hand, I tried to grasp with my other hand anything to stop my fall. Nothing was within reach. I was falling. And falling quickly.

I landed hard on a wooden chute and continued to accelerate. I serpentined down the spiral shaft, faster and faster, rebounding against the sides with my body bouncing back and forth. The rush of damp, stale air flowed past my face. The smell of dank earth and dust filled my lungs. When I thought the ride wouldn't end, I dropped swiftly onto a large pile of wet, sopping hay.

In a dazed and shocked state of semi-consciousness, I raised the lantern to see where I was. I looked around and saw two new shadows standing several meters from me. "Who is there?! Where am I?!"

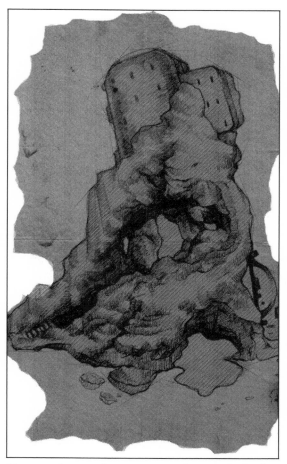

From the unknown reaches of darkness, the mysterious profiles stepped forward into my light to reveal that it was Cristina and Ben. My jaw dropped. I was very confused.

"What are you two doing here!?" I asked with a stern voice.

Shocked and scared, Cristina replied with concern, "I don't know. Where the heck are we?"

Ben continued the questions, "What is this place? We were suddenly dropped in here and can't find the way out."

I placed the lantern down to stand up from the cool, wet ground and tried to move my right leg. My ankle was twisted in an unnatural position. I immediately felt excruciating pain and screamed out loud — a primal scream. "Ouch! I can't get up. My foot, I can't stand. Help me up."

Cristina and Ben approached on each side of me and lifted me up.

Ben offered, "Put your arms around our shoulders. We can lift you up."

I struggled to reach their shoulders. Finally, they lifted me up.

I responded with the obvious, "We need to get out of here. I'm not sure how long I'm going to make it."

Ben shifted his body so I could rest better against him. He said, "It's midnight and there is no one else around the studio. We don't have a lot of options."

Cristina answered with the only logical choice, "Then it will be the three of us who get ourselves out of this mess." She looked at the both of us and then around the room. "Now, where exactly are we?"

The three of us surveyed the room. I looked upwards at the chute that dropped me. "I don't know. I was only visiting the studio, trying to unlock the door. Something was heading down the hallway to get me. And the next thing, the floor disappeared below me and I fell into this ... ah, I don't know what this is or where we are."

Ben clarified my statement with a sense of truth, "No. You were trying to sneak into the studio to find out what Leonardo had hidden." Ben was right.

Cristina explained their predicament, "We've been trapped down here for more than hour. Then you showed up."

"I only wanted to take a quick look into the studio. But I suspect you two had the same goal. So, it was you two who were walking around town in the dark. A stroll under the moonlight?"

Cristina responded, "There is nothing wrong with looking. I don't understand why

Leonardo would use a security device like this."

Ben added, "And a pretty sophisticated security system at that."

I didn't understand everything either. "Whatever he has stored in the studio is so important to him that he wanted those secrets well protected. And he took great measures to see that would happen."

Ben concluded with an obvious assessment, "And we got caught. We were told not to come here and we did it anyway. I am definitely going to lose my apprenticeship."

Cristina looked around the room, moving her head in every which way. "Right now, it is late and we are trapped. There is no way out of here!"

Our tragic midnight meeting had just begun, my ankle was in great pain, and we couldn't give up hope. "If there is a way in, there is a way out. We need to find where that is. We are not going to lose our apprentice-ships or anything else … if we get out of here tonight."

I lifted our sole lantern higher and looked around the cavernous room. What was this place? An old wine cellar or cold storage? I heard stories about Christian catacombs in Florence from my parents, but no one ever found where they were located.

How big was this place? With the little illumination there was in my hands, I limped around the space surveying our situation. We were in an L-shaped room, about ten meters on the long side, and almost five meters on the other side. The sides were a combination of bedrock and hard clay. The wet floor was partially covered in straw, on a foundation of semi-firm clay. Enough for us to make indentations with our footing. The ceilings varied from head height to more than six meters tall.

The chute above us was not easily reachable. But around the corner, there was a thin passageway. This was our only way out at this point. I noticed a small wooden crate near the entrance of the tight walkway. I handed the lantern to Cristina and reached inside. Four rotten apples, a broken wine bottle with a muddy slurry inside, and a leather satchel. The apples were moldy and inedible. The wine undrinkable. So the satchel was our only option.

I unwrapped the straps securing the satchel's contents. Inside was a single page that was slightly ripped and folded twice in half, and a thin stick of graphite for writing.

Ben approached from behind me. "Open it up. What does it say?"

Cristina walked to Ben's side. "Does it show a way out?"

I leaned against the wall and unfolded the page. "It is a map. But it must have gotten wet since it was placed down here. The charcoal markings are smeared at the folds and other areas."

Ben helped me hold the map. We rotated it to establish our orientation, but could not determine where that was.

I spoke up, "We need to survey every wall, corner, and alcove to see if this map was drawn for THIS underground perdition[34]."

Ben and Cristina agreed and the three of us proceeded slowly down the narrow corridor, with Ben providing my necessary walking

---

[34] Perdition → A state of eternal punishment into which a sinful and impenitent person passes after death.

support. Our only hope was to leave our current predicament in search of an exit.

As we moved, Ben counted our paces and Cristina kept track of our directional movements. We encountered several hallways that were dead ends and roundabouts that took us in circles ... to nowhere.

We found ourselves hitting the same passageways, evidenced by seeing our footprint impressions in the clay. We were in an unbelievable maze. If we didn't track our path exactly, we would be revisiting our steps over and over. We had to determine if the map was of any use to us.

After thirty minutes of slowly making our way through the dank labyrinth, one passageway led us to an intersection, a fork in the path.

We paused to evaluate which way to head.

Cristina held out the map as Ben held the lantern. After searching the map's layout and tracing our steps, she reckoned our position and pointed at the map with excitement, "Here, right here. We are at this juncture. See."

Yes, we saw, and all breathed a sigh of relief. My ankle and leg were becoming numb but I pressed forward, determined to escape our unbearable challenge.

From the partially readable map, the right fork seemed to contain more circuitous routes. We decided that the left path was best. We walked about ten paces and found a wooden placard embedded into the wall. It had engraved lettering, but not any letter in any language we understood. We continued and found more placards, each with a different symbolic engraving.

These were runes — marks unknown to us, with some mysterious significance. Their shapes consisted of short, straight lines and arcs; some joined together, some standing alone. Each symbol had a small, solid circle as its companion, placed in no perceivable pattern. Each rune we found was different from the last.

Ben speculated, "These have some significance, but what do they mean?"

At the next turn, we ended up back at the fork we first encountered. We had gone in a full circle.

Cristina took the graphite pencil and map. She formulated a wise plan, "If these runes have meaning, I will keep track of them on this map as we walk this maze." We backtracked and went through other corridors, other offshoots in this maze. Cristina carefully wrote the rune symbols on the map in the location where each was found.

I was starting to get cold, maybe from the chilled air in the caverns and probably because of my injured foot. One route we had not taken during our backtrack was a curved hallway that seemed to never end.

This was when we heard a terrifying sound that made us freeze mid step and sent chills up our spines. An undefinable, screeching sound, like a rusted sword being dragged across a rock. The harsh resonating vibrations changed to a familiar sound, similar to footsteps on a cobble road.

Cristina whispered, "What on Earth was that?"

My heart skipped three beats and my breathing doubled. "I don't know." We had to do something.

Ben moved forward, our newly knighted soldier. "Stay here. I'm going to find out what this thing is. It may get us out of here." I wasn't going to argue. As quickly as he spoke, he ran down the corridor toward the ominous sound. The light of his lantern grew dimmer as Ben chased this monster. His shadow, reflected on the cavern's walls, was getting smaller by the second.

Then the petrifying sound that froze us in our steps vanished as quickly as it came. Cristina and I could still see the faint glow of Ben's lantern. We worked our way slowly toward him down the dark walkway. As we rounded the corner, we reached Ben, who was bent down catching his breath. He was at the end of the corridor.

As we worked our way to Ben, I noticed that the layout of the maze was beginning to make some sense.

Cristina asked our valiant knight, "What happened? What did you find?"

Ben looked at us and griped, "I almost caught up with it. Then suddenly the sound stopped or disappeared. I lost it."

Cristina helped Ben get up.

As Ben caught his breath, I gave them my recent insights, "When we first started out, it seemed like we worked our way outward until we came across this corridor with that awful sound."

Cristina and Ben had my full attention. "This corridor curved much like the outer edge of a circle or an ellipse. If my conclusion is correct, perhaps the exit of the maze does not lie on the outer edge, but rather near its center."

Cristina pulled out the map and traced our last steps. "Yes, you might be right. From what you said, we need to work our way closer to the center."

We gathered ourselves and moved closer to the center. This portion of our journey was not circular, but elliptical. Whatever origins created this labyrinth of confusion, we were resolute to escape its wrath.

The closer we approached the center, the more frequent and louder the screeching and footsteps sounded, only to disappear moments later.

We moved along the corridors, trying to run away from that sound. Ben tripped over some broken wine racks and a couple of disassembled wine barrels. There were no bottles to quench our thirst, which I would have thoroughly enjoyed. With determination and unwavering focus, we paraded forward.

As we approached the next turn, I noticed light at the end of the way. We hadn't been down here long enough that the morning sun might have risen and provided light. It was still night. And besides, we were far underground.

A flash of bright light cycled down from the ceiling, blinding us for a second, followed by a loud thundering sound that echoed against the walls. We moved forward quickly, not waiting for the sights and sounds to intimidate us again.

We reached an underground stream of rushing water. As it had been raining recently the last couple of days, the water level was high and moving quickly. We managed to dredge through the water at knee-height to the other side. As we stepped out of the water, we traversed over a tall mound of stones, almost a perfect cone shaped mound. It was strange to see a collection like this in the cavern. Some of the circular stones seemed to glimmer in a peculiar way. I bent down and picked some of the shiny stones. They were coins. Coins? Why would there be so many stones and then stray coins? I put them in my pocket and moved on.

The passageway opened up into a small elliptical room, several meters in diameter. I hoped our dark journey was close to the end as I was exhausted and had more difficulty walking than before. I immediately took the load off my feet and sat down on the ground.

In excitement, Cristina looked at the map, "This is the end of the maze." Ben and Cristina were jubilant and overjoyed. They hugged each other in comfort and relief that this challenge was over. I wasn't too sure.

The light seemed to be coming from above. The ceiling was very tall and my lantern could not illuminate the entire expanse. This new light was a mystery to me. As my lantern had been the only light source we used before this point, the darkness of the caverns had made my eyes accustomed to the blackness of the underground. This new illumination adversely affected my night vision. I squinted upward to inspect the bright object above. It was round and brilliant with features and gray tones etched within itself.

Cristina peered upwards and also gazed at the bright light. Without any delay, she spouted with confidence, "That's the moon. No question."

How did she know that? I was impressed. I chuckled in agreement, "Wow. Yeah, it's the moon all right."

Ben joined us and looked up with curiosity. "How can you tell?"

I answered slowly, "You can tell by …" Heck, I didn't know.

Cristina saved me, "… The craters all around it. Those lines crisscrossing in front, that's the storm grate near the studio."

"Yeah," I responded with conviction. I learned something new.

The full moon's light reached through the storm grate. This gave me some context to where we were located. It was our first opportunity to get help.

We yelled upwards toward the gridded enclosure, but further flashes of light and large reverberating sounds drowned out our calls. It sounded like lightning and thunder, but on a clear night?

That idea soon revealed itself. The moon's light quickly diminished as clouds covered its valuable glow. Drops of water fell on our heads with increasing intensity. It had started to rain. We were sitting next to the flood channel and needed to move fast.

The flame in our lantern flickered erratically. A coarse gust of wind moved across my face, along with its howling sound flowing past my ears. Rain pelted us from above — faster and faster. The stream grew in size. The weather was changing quickly.

With urgency and not wanting to drown, I quickly scanned the room. In the far corner was a large circular wooden door. At its center was a large bolt that seemed to be resting in front of the door. I got up and inspected it and tried to pull the door open. It wouldn't budge.

The stream was growing bigger. The rushing sound of water buffeted the walls and floor. Ben yelled to me, "We need to get out of here now! Water is pouring down from the ceiling and rising fast!"

I looked over and Ben and Cristina were soaked. I yelled back, "Get over here. I need your help!"

Cristina and Ben joined me immediately and we worked on our exit solution. There were two poles at its center. They acted as guiders for the bolt. I instructed them with eminent urgency, "Slide these poles away from each other!" Water started to rise above our ankles. If we didn't complete this task in the next minute, the water pressure would hold the door closed and we would be submerged under the rising water. Trapped.

With a sudden jerk and thrust, we moved the poles in opposing directions. But as we moved them further away, resistance quickly built up. We had to muster all we had to slide the pole through, enough to clear the way for the door to be opened. We hurried as fast as we could.

Cristina yelled in desperation, "MORE! Push harder!"

The damp conditions provided unneeded friction between the poles and the guides for the bolt. With a final shove, the poles latched and locked in place. Success! We unlocked the door.

The three of us pulled the door open, enough to permit ourselves to exit. At that moment, triggered by the open passageway, a rush of wind charged from the ceiling above and flowed through our exit way, creating a relentless gale of rain and wind. The door opening had transformed itself into a conduit for a powerful ventilation tunnel. If we didn't act quickly, we would be sucked forward and the door would slam with great force and crush us.

Amidst the growing torrent of wind and spray of water, Ben shouted, "You two go through! I'll hold the door!"

Time was critical. Without hesitation, Cristina helped me as I limped and quickly passed through the door. The wind picked up speed, becoming fiercer. I yelled, "We're through! Come on!"

Looking back at Ben, I noticed a shadowy figure approach him — and grab his body. It was the same shadow I had seen earlier up in the hallway.

The dark silhouette called out in a loud, emphatic yell, "NOOOO! Come back! Stay here!"

Ben struggled to get free from the shadow's grasp and still hold the door. Both impedements were relentless in their determination to force Ben one way or another. But not both.

Finally, the water and force of air was too strong. Ben moved to our side of the large circular door and without notice, the door slammed closed, which launched Ben — and the shadow — flying unpredictably forward toward where we stood.

With a loud thud, the door shut with great force, stopping the gale force winds that prompted our quick escape.

Cristina helped Ben while I lay next to the shadow, our new member of the group. I looked at his face. He was one of the men I had seen at Leonardo's door the other day.

I quickly backed away from him. "Who are you? And why did you follow us?" He seemed shaken from the fall and was slowly getting his bearings.

I checked on the door through which we had come. There were no handles. I pushed with all my strength. The door would not budge. It had locked when the door slammed shut.

We could not go back the way we came. But did we escape? I looked around and determined that it was no escape. We were still trapped. And now with a new piece introduced into our puzzle.

CHAPTER 12 - MENDING FENCES AND THE GUEST

Cristina and I were both emotionally and physically exhausted from our narrow escape, thanks to Ben. But he was not okay. He lay on the ground in a contorted position, not moving. Cristina attended to him, straightening out his legs and arms, raising his head on her lap. She cleared dirt and debris from his face and hair. "He's breathing. Slowly."

Our new guest sat up and moved against the cold clay wall. He looked very familiar; he was one of the men who had moved the crates into Leonardo's studio. A balding, short, beefy guy whose whiskers could be used as sandpaper. His blemished, weather-beaten face looked like the cratered roads leading around Florence. His tiny fingers were equally rough, gnarled, and very knobby. He appeared to be a hefty man who has had a rugged life and who just raised our level of anxiety within this challenging labyrinth.

He repositioned his legs and shifted his torso. We made motionless eye contact for several seconds. He spoke with a soft, gravelly voice, "What are you kids doing down here? You do not belong here."

Kids? I closed my eyes and took a deep breath to regain my confident yet slightly ruffled composure. I responded assertively, "We are not kids. We are apprentices to Leonardo da Vinci."

"Why did you go through this door? You would have been safe if you stayed with me. Now we are tossed into this new part that I do not know."

"Why did you chase me up in the hallway?"

"I was trying to save you from falling into this mess! Leonardo said to check on his studio and make sure all was safe. When I saw someone at the door, I knew he wasn't supposed to be there. I could ask the same for all three of you."

"You were at the studio the other day. Who are you?"

"I'm Lorenzo. I've known Leonardo for many years. I help him now and then with his

experiments … moving them here and there."
He looked over at Cristina and Ben, "Now the
three of you are not where you want to be. I
don't know much about these other parts of
the cavern." Lorenzo rested his head back
against the wall and took a deep breath.

Our uninvited guest presented a new
wrinkle. He could tell Leonardo and ruin our
apprenticeship, employment, and future as
artists. Maybe we could pay him to keep quiet
or to promise not to tell. We would need to
figure out how to deal with that later. The
challenge at hand was to get out of this place
— alive and in one piece.

I moved toward Ben and knelt by his side,
holding his hand, "Ben. Ben, wake up. Wake
up."

We sat there for a couple of minutes
helping Ben, wondering if we would ever get
out. What additional trouble had we gotten
ourselves into? We only wanted to satisfy our
curiosity and find out what was hidden in the
studio. Not this.

I closed my eyes for a moment to try and
figure out what we could do next. These
people in front of me were no longer fellow
apprentices. They were my friends, one of

whom risked his life for us. They both had good hearts — and I hadn't apologized to them. If we were going to continue our quest, we would need to work together without apprehension. We needed to renew our relationship and fix what was broke.

I looked over at Cristina and smiled at her. "Thank you for helping me … for helping us out. I'm sorry for what I said yesterday. I had no right to discredit Ben or you, or each of your awe-inspiring talents."

Cristina smiled back and started to cry. "I'm sorry, too. Both you and Ben are great friends and great artists. Things got out of hand and our emotions got the best of us. We are better than that."

I reached over and wiped her tears away. "There. We will get out of here. We've gotten this far. Ben was Herculean in his effort, holding that door for us. He is a great friend to both of us. He saved our lives."

Ben moaned and gradually moved his fingers. With his eyes still closed and still groggy, Ben spoke, "Hmm, those hands I'm holding … they are soft and smooth. Either the hands of a fantastic sculptor or those of a demanding architect."

We all started to laugh uncontrollably. Ben opened his eyes and looked at us. "That is the last time I do something stupid like that. Unless, of course, I need to save both of you." We continued to laugh, a good, needed laugh.

Ben looked over at the man resting on the wall. "Who is that? Was that who was trying to pull me back?"

"Yeah. His name is Lorenzo. He is a friend of Leonardo. For some reason, he followed us down here and tried to ... help us."

Ben called out, "HEY! LORENZO! What the hell were you trying to do? You almost got me killed."

Lorenzo raised his head and responded in a calm voice, "You'll be okay, young man. Just a bruise here and there. Just a little waterlogged."

Cristina chimed in, looking at Ben and our guest, "Well, Mr. Lorenzo, you may enjoy the water but ... I can't swim. I am glad to be on this side of the door." Cristina looked over at Ben and laughed. "Yeah, did I ever tell you I couldn't swim? I really didn't want to hold that door. I'm glad Ben offered." We laughed further. The tension we created the day before had disappeared.

I added, "Thank you, Ben. If we hadn't gotten out of there, we would have been trapped ... and died."

"We are okay. All of us. Just a few scratches and bumps for our efforts, that's all." Ben changed positions and stretched his limbs. "Ouch, I think I'm going to be feeling this for several days."

"I am sorry to have spoken out like I did to both of you. I was out of place and what I said was totally inappropriate. Art is many things to many people. Anything that is important to you is important to me. Please accept my apology."

Cristina provided her apology, "I am sorry. I had no right disrespecting both of your talents and passions. You are great guys and friends. Please forgive my ignorance." She bowed her head in shame.

Cristina and I then looked at Ben, awaiting his response. He looked up and coughed and smiled. "Okay, I'm guilty, too. Both of you are wonderful artists and have creative talents for which I am speechless. Your work inspires me to learn and understand a side of art which I don't fully appreciate."

I added, "I think we all have gifts that we can share with each other. Among friends. When I got home last night, I was drenched."

The others spoke and chuckled at the same time, "Me too."

"But I knew both of you were good people. And I want to continue that friendship."

Cristina spoke up, "You are my best friends, my … true friends."

Our friendships were mended. Of course, it would have been nicer to have done so under better circumstances.

Ben raised his head and looked at us. "Okay, young apprentices, I have a great idea. What do you say we get back to business, back to work, and get out of this place?"

We all agreed.

CHAPTER 13 - THE GENEVA WHEEL

Both Cristina and I helped Ben stand up. He was able to walk and move around, albeit somewhat slowly at first.

Lorenzo stood up and joined us. "I'm sorry, guys, I don't remember this segment as much. In fact, none of it looks familiar. It has been several years."

I looked around the room and noticed we had entered into another chamber in this maze. It was not the exit I had hoped. The water that entered through the door had dissipated into the corners of the space, which was about six meters in all directions. The further reaches of the room were a lot drier and warmer, but more excitingly, there was a passageway into another space.

Still somewhat soaked, Cristina pulled out the wet map to see where we were. Opening it carefully and slowly so as not to tear it further, she figured out that the door we had traveled through was at the edge of the map. There was nothing else after that point.

The path to the next room had a slight change in elevation and was dotted with boulders and rock debris. Cristina led the way with the lantern while Ben and I helped each other navigate through the maze. Lorenzo seemed to be on his own, navigating his way forward. He would look back at us often, but then continue on. When we reached the opening to the room, I was exhausted.

Lorenzo cleared the rocks next to me so I could sit. Ben seemed to have recovered a little more from his earlier fall. I was very glad. I would feel terrible if anything happened to any of us — including Lorenzo.

Ben spied a place to sit, but what looked like a flat rock turned out to be a second satchel — this one covered in a thick layer dirt and stones. Ben dusted off the bag, which created a pillow of dust that lingered around our heads. "Sorry about that," he said as we all coughed out three layers of muck. He opened the satchel and found another map.

Ben gazed at the map for a second and then looked at us. He wiped the dirt from his mouth and spit to the ground. "Hmm, wow! A map. So we are trapped down here and the only thing that comes to our defense is another measly map. That leads us on a wild goose chase. No tools. No ladders. No magic door that leads us out. Just another map."

I leaned in and put my hand on Ben's shoulder. "It's okay. Really. It is what it is. This is all we have and need to make the best of it."

Cristina looked closer between the two maps and noticed a strange similarity. She cleared her throat and provided some encouragement, "Now, this new map is altogether different, but the door and room from our first map is also on this map. It is a continuation. Great! We have a point of reference."

Ben placed his hand on his head. "Okay, okay," he yielded. "Another round of challenges. Let's see what this map has to say."

As Ben and Cristina surveyed the map, Lorenzo and I looked around the room. It seemed significantly larger — ten to fifteen meters wide. It was hard to tell as the light from our lantern bounced and reflected across all the walls and floor. I could not see any other passageways leading out of the room.

The ceiling seemed a lot taller than the other room, yet I could not see its roof. This large chamber seemed like a dead end.

Cristina pointed to the map and then looked into the room, "The map shows another corridor past this room, but it's too dark to see it here." She held the map and walked forward as the three of us men followed.

The lantern illuminated two semi-circular wooden platforms, one on the floor and one perpendicular to it against the wall. Measuring about a couple of meters in diameter, the platform at our feet contained a tall pole anchored at its base that traveled through to the ceiling. Connected to the pole adjacent to the wall at waist height was a gear. This drive mechanism was coupled to a strange looking center wheel on the wall.

We inspected the area from all angles to understand what the mechanism did. We raised the lantern higher, which lit up several features on the surface of the wall. First was a set of six moderate-sized discs arranged around the center disc. Each disc was about the size of my outspread hand, thumb to little-finger — about six or seven inches. The discs cast a strange golden tinge when light shined upon them.

Next was the surface of the wall, which was a plane of several interconnected and recessed chasms, small fissures about half the width of a small finger. They followed a central arc-like path around the vertical plane of the wall. All composed on this large, semi-circular wheel.

I looked closer at the device. "Whatever this large apparatus is, or does, it is our only choice at the moment. I think we need to decipher its meaning to solve this puzzle." I glanced over to Lorenzo, "Do you know what this is or how to work it?"

Lorenzo shook his head. "Sorry, I can't help you out here."

Ben responded in a frustrated tone, "What other choice do we have? Let's figure this out."

As Ben reached to move the closest golden disc, the pole began to turn. Starting out slow, its movement made a loud grinding sound. At the base, the pole ground itself against a small indentation in the floor. After about eight rotations, the pole stopped. Nothing happened. Its effect on the wheel and discs did nothing. We didn't know if the pole and its

gears were supposed to control the mechanisms on the wall.

Ben continued and moved the golden disc
along the path in one fissure. As he did,
Cristina and I noticed that it had a small gear
attached to its base, as did the rest of the discs.
Not all of the gears were the same size —
some appeared larger while others appeared
much smaller. The whole assembly looked very
familiar.

I remembered about seven years ago one
summer when my father and I visited Rome
and met a clock and watchmaker, Frater Franza
Baccarat, a German Augustinian friar from the
city of Augsburg in Bavaria. He was in Rome
within the Papal court of Pope Sixtus IV
delivering several unusual clocks and watches.
The variety of complex designs and detailing
was magnificent.

As a young boy, I was fascinated with
intricate designs and mechanical devices.
Franza showed us the inner workings of a
spring powered clock and explained how it
worked. His clock had a series of small,
interconnected gears that worked together to
move the hands. The mainspring or some
other force had a mechanism to allow it to be

wound up. The barrel had gear teeth on it, which drove the center balance wheel. All meticulously assembled to tell the time of day.

Before mechanical clocks existed, water clocks had been used for thousands of years. These types of clocks measured time by the regulated flow of liquid into or out of a vessel where the amount was then measured.

I inspected the discs and channels more closely and noticed that not only did they have some very interesting designs, they also had a lot gears that were connected in some way, like a clock's gears. Something told me that this apparatus in front of us was possibly the creation of our master, Leonardo da Vinci.

I held the lantern up closer to the platform and peered inside. "Here, take a look inside this channel. You can see smaller gears behind there are connected to other gears. This is very much like how a clock functions. I am pretty sure that this pole provides energy to move those inner gears, like a mainspring." I anxiously awaited the next movement of the pole to prove my assumption.

Continuing on, Cristina shifted a different disc along another opening. After observing these movements, I saw that the disc gears traveled along the channels and possibly slid into specific spots located sporadically throughout the space. However, the discs would not move by the simple act of pushing them; that is, until Cristina realized they were already partially inserted into the wall. Pulling them proved to be practically effortless.

Once we determined the operational nature of the gears, they slid easily along the paths until they dropped into the next opening. This challenge proved to be easier than we thought. For one, we didn't have to walk a multitude of passageways, or get soaked and blown by torrential weather forces. What would happen when we solved this challenge?

Repeating every few minutes, the pole rotated again, clockwise like before, turning the interconnected gears. Since we had moved the discs, the pole's movement struggled.

Ben placed his hands on the gear and the corresponding wheel on the wall. "I can feel the pressure building against these pieces. I'm not sure they can take this stress much more."

Holding the lantern up close to the mechanism, I could see the gears starting to contort out of shape. They were under a great amount of strain. Every time the pole moved, it restricted our attempts to move the gears. When the pole stopped moving, we were able to continue. The pole and gears were designed to work together — for a specific purpose. Over time, these parts would warp and weaken. If either part on this wall broke, we would be stuck. We couldn't go back the way we came. The only option was to see this through.

I spoke up with a sense of urgency. "The pole is trying to turn or activate something on the wall. If it breaks, we … we need to hurry!"

We continued at a faster pace. Not every gear, though, fell into place properly, and it took a great deal of experimentation to finally figure out where each gear fit correctly. Cristina, Ben, and I took turns and slid gears into place. We moved more quickly with each motion. As a team, we achieved a certain rhythm and cadence that would make Leonardo happy. If this crazy contrivance broke, we would never be able to tell him or anyone our story.

Amidst our frantic and calculated movements, just before Cristina slid the last disc into place, the pole started to turn — freezing any movement of that disc.

We needed just a few more seconds for the turn of the pole, but our concentration was abruptly interrupted again. The horrifying sound from before returned. This time it moved for a few seconds, then stopped, then resumed.

All the while, the pole was trying, struggling to rotate. Ben and Cristina struggled to move the last disc into place. It wouldn't budge. I looked around to see what the noise was.

That was when Ben noticed two glowing orbs hovering at about waist high. Instead of being stationary though, they were moving and soon took on the shape of illuminated eyes.

Cristina yelled, "Oh my God!" There was no place for us to hide. We had to stay there to move the disc when the pole stopped moving.

The orbs were headed right for us! Six meters away and moving quickly. The heck with this pole! I placed my hands on the disc and shouted out, "ALL TOGETHER, push the disc … NOW!"

We thrust our bodies against the disc gear and slammed it into place. I hoped that we didn't break it. I hoped that the gears were finally in their correct place.

As we ducked for protection in a group huddle, covering ourselves from the descending orbs, the pole turned the gears, which turned the center wheel. I felt the entire platform rumble where we cowered. The platform rotated very quickly, like a round table revolving in a circle. The entire mechanism and the three of us turned with it — 180 degrees. Away from the attacking orbs and their villainous-looking eyes.

The platform suddenly stopped its rotation, which sent deep and intense reverberations trembling through our bodies. We were safe. Away from any harm. For the moment.

What I didn't understand was Lorenzo. Had he only visited part of the labyrinth years before? Why? Was he trying to sneak into Leonardo's studio? Did he not get this far to understand how this rotating platform worked? I was going to find out. If he knows anything that can help us, he'd better share that information. The pain in my ankle was increasing and I didn't know what was going to happen. We needed to get out of this place.

CHAPTER 14 - THE NEVER-ENDING PATH

Our level of anxiety had reached its peak in our journey through these complex challenges, yet we retained a strong determination to escape and an equally strong desire to live to be a year older. But my injured ankle was beginning to fail me. Every step I took came with increased pain. This started to slow us down. I didn't want to be a burden to Cristina, Ben, or Lorenzo.

After our last trial, I tried to move independently through this new set of passageways without complaining. I covered up facial grimaces and spasms in my foot without them noticing. I let them lead the way with assurances that I was right behind.

It must have been about three or four o'clock in the morning at this point. Had

Giovanna wondered why I didn't catch up to her? Were my parents and those of Cristina and Ben also worried? Why had we not returned home? Had my parents been over to Giovanna's house to check if I was there? Niccolo and Serena were fast asleep with no idea what encounters we had been through or what awaited around the next bend. Anyone eventually finding us dead was not an option I wanted to offer.

I walked up to Lorenzo and tried to keep pace with the whole group. "When did you come down here? How long has it been?"

"It was many years ago, when I was in my twenties. My friends and I were loading empty wine barrels for a vintner[35] into a part of these caverns. While we were resting, I went to take a pee and found a boarded-up area. I called my friends and we opened up the boards and explored the many passageways. We got lost and became frantic trying to find out way out. We finally got out but I was scared out of my wits and vowed to never do that again. But here I am."

"And here you are. Don't you remember these passages? Anything?"

---

[35] <u>Vintner</u> → A winemaker.

"I'm so sorry, I wish I could help you out."

We walked through a narrow tunnel for about thirty or forty minutes, taking breaks to rest along the way. If our lantern ran out of oil, we would be forever consumed in the darkness that haunted our presence and hope. Without food or water, our energy levels were slowly diminishing. The support and encouragement, and sometimes laughter, that we gave each other helped us move toward a future outside of this cavern.

I wondered how far we had traveled with all the twists and turns. Some access ways seemed to make complete circles, going up and down small dark banks. Yet the snake-like weaving through the tunnels never resulted in revisiting the same path.

CHAPTER 15 - THE PARADOX SLIDERS

With Ben at the lead, we pressed forward down a narrow corridor, squeezing our torsos between jagged rock and cold damp clay. Lorenzo walked next to Cristina and helped her navigate the challenging path.

Lorenzo told us stories of his childhood and teenage years. He talked about walking on the ice of the Arno River during winter with his friends, finding their favorite spot, sawing a hole, and fishing for hours. "My three best friends and I enjoyed ice fishing. Though that day the temperature was warmer, we set up a fire on the bank of the river so we could warm our cold feet and hands, and importantly be ready for frying fish later. There was about a half inch of water on top of the ice, so any time you cut a hole, the water was going to be running in it. So you have to keep an eye on how big your hole is because it would wear it away. We brought wooden crates to sit on while we fished.

"Because of the layer of water on top of the ice, we were careful not to get our shoes too wet. The depth of the ice was okay for our combined weight as we measured it to be about five to eight inches thick. That was safe enough for us. After about an hour of fishing, I walked around to see how my friends were doing. I was acting reckless for my teenage years and tried to jump from one part of the hole's edge to the other. My feet slipped and I fell straight into the water. And I didn't know how to swim. I quickly surfaced and my friends pulled me out. I got undressed and my friends shared their clothing for me. We sat around the fire, warmed up, and fried our catch of the day.

"These guys saved my life and I will never forget what they did. To this day, I keep in touch with them and their families. Our friendship is very special."

From what Lorenzo described, I saw my relationship with Cristina and Ben in the same way — a fellowship of friends. I hoped that our time down here would end and we could continue our lives together in the world above.

After about fifteen minutes, the passageway opened up into yet another open chamber. The ceiling towered high above, with irregular and uneven rock formations riding up the ominous fortification.

We looked around for any sign of another map. Something that may have been left to show a way out. Nothing was in sight. This time, the challenge in front of us was going to be accomplished on our own. We had no idea how many challenges there were left. Was this the last one? Were we close to the end?

Surrounding the room were several picture frames of different sizes mounted at various heights and distances apart from each other. There were no pictures mounted within the frames.

Ben looked around the room and offered his humorous insights, "Let's see, there are more than a dozen frames here awaiting a magnificent painting for each. This is not normal. I could easily produce some awe-inspiring and impressive paintings in a week's time. Then sell them from my *botteghe*[36] storefront for a good wage."

Cristina looked at him and smiled, "Yes, and I as the studio's master would pay you a small commission for your work." We all had a good laugh for that moment. A reprieve that lessened the stress.

At the center of the room, dividing it in half was a bridge-like structure very similar to an aqueduct. The bridge provided passageway across a wide and deep crevasse. Without any handrails, the structure arched above the ground and was almost a meter wide and nine to ten meters in length. It was too wide to jump across without the bridge. I would not be able make such a leap.

The path across was not passable as there were twelve huge vertical and diagonal wooden posts arranged to block any passage, with no room to skirt to either side. Written on each post was a single letter.

Positioned to the left of the bridge were a series of six thin boards with archaic-like runes, like we had seen before, etched on them. Each board acted as a slide that went underneath the

---

[36] <u>Botteghe</u> → A place of work of an artist and his potential apprentices.

bridge. The same number of boards was on the right side. Twelve boards and twelve posts. This was probably not a coincidence.

Ben and I analyzed the structure from all sides. Cristina moved one slide forward, which moved one of the posts on the bridge downward, though not completely down. She moved a second slide and another post rose higher.

I provided my expert architectural assessment to the group, "These boards seem to work in conjunction with the runes. Perhaps moving all twelve sliders into a different placement would change the post's orientation enough to allow us to pass." That seemed like a worthy proposition to try.

I felt bad we hadn't included Lorenzo in any of our deliberations. He was strong and seemed smart enough to figure out — or at least try and figure out — some of these obstacles. "Hey Lorenzo, what do you think we can do here? Any ideas?"

Lorenzo walked up to the bridge and peered over to the picture frames. "I don't know. I think this situation needs more brain than brawn."

Cristina and Ben started to work on the sliders, moving them to and fro and trying multiple random configurations. I watched the bridge and noticed no significant change in the height or position of the posts. The odds of chancing upon the correct order were infinitesimally small. I noticed that the runes on the sliders and letters on the posts followed a specific pattern. There was a correlation between the two.

Ben and Cristina took a break and sat on the ground to rest. It had definitely been a long night. Ben leaned forward and put his hands behind his head and closed his eyes. I stood up on my good foot and started combining letters in descending order, trying to form some sort of phrase or sentence that might tell how the sliders were to be ordered correctly. And what was with the frames on the wall? What was their significance?

Ben and Cristina's break and my concentration were interrupted again by the sound of metallic footsteps, fading in and out. The sounds echoed in the chamber and we could not determine where or how close this — thing — was. We were definitely not alone. But whatever it was, we hadn't been harmed by it yet.

With intense focus, shutting out any distractions, I gazed back to the floor where my eyes and fingers magically drifted and pointed over four letters. I quietly and slowly annunciated them out loud: "U-L-T-I."

Ben raised his head and interrupted me with excitement, "… M-A! The picture frames! It's the picture frames. U-L-T-I … -M-A!, *Ultima! Ultima Manus*[37]. That is what Leonardo has been saying to us. Do you remember? Dream. Design, Sketch, Create."

Ben explained with a passion, a renewed drive, I had not seen while we were in these caverns.

He stood up and joined me. "The final touch, the final step after seeing our idea, our work, our creation, all the way through to the end, is putting it on display. Framing the masterpiece. Like in a picture frame. *Ultima Manus.*

Cristina looked over and gave Ben a gleaming smile. A sense of hope had just revealed itself.

---

[37] *Ultima Manus* → Latin for "The last hand; the final touch."

Pausing as he thought to himself, Ben counted with his fingers. *Ultima Manus* has eleven letters. But there are twelve sliders."

Cristina stood up and joined us. She pointed to the sliders. "What is the twelfth letter?" She looked at the entire suite of letters. "Look, a slider with no symbol on it. A blank space! Used between words. Two words. Our words."

Ben replied energetically, "Yes!"

With renewed enthusiasm and all of us pointing to each of the sliders in order, we spoke in unison: "U-L-T-I-M-A space! M-A-N-U-S. *Ultima Manus*!"

It had taken an exhausted Ben to get us back on track again. We were very happy, reinvigorated, and ready to solve this puzzle. The three of us immediately began pushing the sliders into place, spelling out the two words in precise letter order. With each movement, the posts dropped down completely.

Cristina moved the last slider and the final post moved out of the way. Full access to the bridge was ready for its anxious passengers.

Cristina looked confused. "That was strange. This slider moved differently from the others. I feel a lot of tension on this one." She lifted her hand off the slider and it sprang back into its place. And the post rose back up, which automatically released back all the other posts. The posts had been reset. Passageway over the bridge was impossible.

Ben and Cristina moved the sliders again, in order. When Cristina got to the last slider, she held it in place. She tried placing a rock on the slider but the force moved it away. She caught the slider before it returned to its original position. "We have a serious problem."

Lorenzo walked up and held Cristina's slider in place. "No, you don't. Go. The three of you, go. Head over the bridge and continue on. I'm okay here. When you get out, you can come back for me."

Cristina put her arm around Lorenzo. "You remind me of my dad when I was young. He was strong and tall. He would play with me, tossing me up in the air. He would kiss me on the cheek and move his mustache back and forth. He knew that it would make me laugh. He made me feel good. He was always very thoughtful and would do anything for me." A tear dropped down her cheek. "We'll come back, I promise." She gave him a kiss on the cheek. "Thank you."

Ben came over and shook Lorenzo's other hand. "Thank you, sir. I'm sorry it worked out this way. We'll be back for you."

I came and gave Lorenzo a hug. "Grazie, Lorenzo. Grazie."

Lorenzo gave us all a huge smile. "Okay, okay. I'll be waiting for you. Now, go."

We crossed over the bridge; Ben was first, eager to move onward. Cristina was next. I followed, holding her hand for balance as I limped across and navigated my way. I didn't look down into the abyss, but trusted my dangling footsteps as I steered them, inch by inch, toward the other side.

When we reached the other side, Lorenzo released the slider and the posts returned to their position.

Cristina called out, "We'll be back. We will get out."

Holding each other's hands, the three of us quietly walked out of the room. We would be back.

CHAPTER 16 - THE CRYPTEX

I could sense that Ben and Cristina's nerves were on edge. We had been up since dawn the day before and then had been exposed to the labyrinth's physical and mental challenges. We were on the brink of collapse. Yet we pushed forward, almost like soul-less corpses, zapped of all energy. We were more than tired and began questioning our purpose down here.

Leonardo may have had good intentions to capture or retain thieves at his studio by devising this maze, but to unfold these creative obstacles on unsuspecting apprentices was having its wear on us. Could we ever look at him any differently and still have respect for the man?

The three of us trudged ahead, our confidence waning, in hope that the end would be near. We came across a split passageway, a fork in the road. The last map had run its course. Should we go left or right?

My foot was pretty much useless. Ben helped me stand at this point. With a lantern in hand, Cristina scoped out the right passageway while we waited.

As she walked down about ten meters away, Ben and I could see something suddenly illuminate the end of the passageway. It wasn't Cristina's lantern; it was something else.

She headed back and gave us a status, "There IS something ahead. A light turned on. I didn't want to go too far without both of you."

Ben answered with an elevated voice of optimism, "Yes, we saw it, too."

Cristina quickly replied, "I think that is the way we should go."

Ben was anxious to proceed down that corridor.

I asked both of them, "Before we try that, can we do a quick check of the left passageway? I know we are tired, but I think we should be careful and on guard with whatever choice we make."

I inspected the lantern and shook it to see how much oil was left. There was nothing inside the base. "I don't know how much longer we have. The oil in here is empty. It's all in the wick. Maybe five or ten minutes, or less." I set the lantern down so I could sit and rest my foot.

Ben spoke up with a sense of urgency, "I am way too tired and I'm not waiting to see if one way is better than the next. This way looks as good as any. Cristina found light and for me, that's the hope I've been waiting for. I'm heading in that direction."

Cristina picked up the lantern and started walking down the right passageway with Ben. "I'm tired and need to get out of this place. Lorenzo is counting on us. Come on, Francesco. Let's go. We will walk slowly."

They proceeded down the corridor ahead of me. As they rounded one corner, their lantern light started to diminish.

Cristina called back in excitement, "I see more light up ahead! Multiple colors, like the stained glass at the church."

Ben followed up, "Hurry up, Francesco. We'll wait for you at this next area." I stood up and worked my way toward their light. They had placed the lantern down so I could see it as I approached.

I felt alone without them, but didn't want to lessen their enthusiasm and new-found energy. We had gone through enough tonight.

Cristina called out again, "THIS IS IT! There are prisms and mirrors just like in Leonardo's studio."

I rounded the corner and reached the lantern. They were four meters in front of the light.

Ben spoke up, "These prisms are reflecting light from somewhere."

He reached out and moved one of the prisms. At that moment, a large weighted gate slammed down behind them, blocking any retreat. The sound of the gate crashing down resounded throughout the cavern.

I hurried and approached the gate that now stood between me and my friends. The three of us tried to lift up this new, unwelcome barrier. After a minute of exerting all we had left in us, the gate would not budge. It was too heavy. We tried several times, working at different angles and looking everywhere for any objects to use as leverage.

Cristina noticed a hook on the outside of the gate where I stood. I tried to reach it by straddling the horizontal bars weaved along the gate. I grabbed the hook and hung on to it, dangling my feet away from the gate. My weight was not enough to pull it down.

I worked my footing back to the gate and stepped down to the ground. My hands were sore and calloused. I dropped to my knees, exhausted.

Worn out and weary, Cristina approached the gate with her head resting against the bars, "Francesco, we're stuck here. There's no way to move this thing. Leave us and see if you can get yourself out. Try the other passageway."

The looks on their faces revealed exhaustion and desperation. I, too, was ready to collapse. But this was not the end for either of us. "I won't go on without you two. There has to be a way to lift this gate."

Ben approached the cold steel bars, "We tried and there isn't. We will be okay. There is another way. Just not this way. Go back and see where the other passage takes you."

I stood up and joined them at the gate. We comforted each other, holding each other's hands as true friends.

I picked up the lantern and stumbled awkwardly back to the fork.

Ben called out, "Be careful, Francesco. You can do it."

I glanced back. "I will. I will return with help."

I reached the fork and walked on the virgin passage before turning around a bend. I lifted the lantern in front of me and stopped in my tracks. I had discovered my next challenge. I walked forward to closely inspect this colossal device.

There was a huge cylindrical column about three meters wide and ten meters high with steps going up and around the pillar. The column was split into eight separate and con-nected segments, stacked onto this tower. Starting at the base, every other tier was encircled with a large number of runes with one deep hole. The sections between the rune layers had only letters etched.

The entrance to the stairs was blocked with a simple pole attached to the left and right posts of the stairs.

I remembered a week back, Leonardo had talked about creating a cypher-enabled tubular vault to hide secret messages or anything that you would want kept protected. He showed us a miniature he made that was encoded with rotating discs and letters. This Cryptex, as he called it, when unlocked properly, would release an inside channel revealing the secret item. Nearly unsolvable unless the user knew the pre-set code.

The monolith in front of me was certainly comparable to what he had shown. But this one had the same blasted runic language inscribed on it. The question was: What was the proper combination?

I limped around the base of the structure to examine every aspect of its being, looking at every rune to figure out what it meant and how to apply its language toward a solution.

Out of the corner of my eye, from above, I saw two bright lights paired together, coming toward me. Then that metallic screeching noise reintroduced its ugly sound.

I was tired, agitated, and sick of this thing charging us — and now me. I grabbed the pole at the stairway entrance and was going to fight this time. I yelled out loud, "Whatever doesn't kill me ... had better start running!"

As the menace got closer, I raised my pole, my makeshift sword, in a defensive posture.

The unknown threat was itself now in danger. When it was within striking distance, I swung my makeshift saber and struck it face on. I detached its body from the long cable it was using to swipe down on me. The tether had fully severed from its connection points above and lay motionless in front of me. I approached the body slowly with my lantern raised high in one hand and sword in the other. Any further movement and it was history.

I stepped closer. It was a contorted framework of wooden construction: a cart. One of the drawings in Leonardo's studio matched what lay before me: a mechanical pulley system and self-propelled cart. I wondered if the rotating pole we had discovered earlier provided the energy to move the cable and the cart from place to place. If so, it didn't anymore. At least, not this one. But, were there more of these flying carts hiding around another corner? Had this cart been following us all this time? Either way, I was ready to swing again.

I looked closer at the wooden wreck. The eyes of the cart came from two concave mirrors positioned in front to direct the light emitted from the two small lanterns. A large reservoir of oil in the cart powered the lanterns via a metal feed. The lights were not broken in the attack.

I don't think there was any intelligence driving its offensives. It had probably been riding around these caverns, awaiting someone to gracefully stop it or for itself to eventually break down. I introduced a third option: an unfortunate malfunction.

Having defended my honor, I traveled back to Cristina and Ben to relay everything I found — and destroyed.

Ben and Cristina had heard the noise from a distance and could not tell if I was injured or dead. The site of me relieved their concern.

Ben spoke up, "We heard that noise and crash, and didn't know what to expect. What happened?"

I told them the annoyance was probably one of Leonardo's inventions and that I had disabled it with some good physical attention: cart, cable, and all.

I mentioned finding a large Cryptex structure and presented my assessment, "It seems like the four cylinders are connected in some way, with runes inscribed around all its sides. I think each of the four layers are related to each challenge we have experienced so far. The problem is, I don't remember the exact runes and solutions we discovered."

Ben mentioned he didn't remember exactly either. We were rushed through each event and the details were unclear.

Cristina spoke up, "Oh, I don't remember exactly what we did either, but that's okay." She turned around and knelt to the ground. She picked up the two maps and presented them to me. "I believe these maps might help.

They don't tell you what we did and won't help much. But my notes on the other side might."

I turned the maps over and was delighted to see notations from each of the challenges in remarkable detail.

She continued, "I took the liberty to jot down some key notes. I hope you don't mind." This was the comic relief we needed. The three of us started laughing and applauded Cristina.

Looking over her notes, we discussed the various attributes for each solution we had used earlier in the evening — how the runes aligned with the letters for each level in the Cryptex.

We reasoned that the four-letter word that was associated with the four Cryptex rune levels was: "*Velo*[38]," which was the fundamental purpose of the Cryptex: to hide a secret inside by wrapping it up. I hoped our deduction was correct.

With renewed hope, I returned to the Cryptex and reviewed the map notes on the first puzzle for the specific rune I needed to align. I knew the first segment of the Cryptex needed to be moved, but didn't have the strength to rotate it by itself. There must be a

---

[38] <u>Velo</u> → Latin for "I hide by wrapping something up."

way to pivot each section. I walked around
again to see what could be used and noticed
the indentations in the section: runes and … an
indentation presenting a deep hole. I grabbed
the pole I had used to destroy the cart and
pushed it into the cavity. When fully inserted, I
heard it click into place.

With two hands on the pole, I easily rotated
the section around to the proper position,
aligning the rune up with the corresponding
letter immediately above: V. This was going to
be easy if we were right.

As soon as the first rune layer aligned with
the lettered-layer above, a level of panels above
the two layers opened up and a rush of wind
knocked me over. The notes slipped out of my
hands and flew away. Engaging the first
solution must have activated something in the
Cryptex to channel wind through it. And the
Cryptex cylinder started to rotate clockwise,
making any further movements extremely
difficult. The wind force got stronger with each
passing second, so I needed to pick up my
pace.

I looked over at the rotating column and
had an idea. I picked up one end of the severed
cable and returned to Ben and Cristina's

temporary jail. The pressure of the wind as I limped down that corridor was unbearable and made it difficult to stand as it pushed me from behind. I grabbed on to the wall to help balance myself.

When I reached them, I graciously offered, "I told you I would bring help." I created a loop on the cable and climbed up the gate. Ben reached up and helped me to secure the loop onto the hook.

When I let go of the cable and reached for the bars, I lost my footing on the gate and quickly descended downward. At mid-fall, Ben and Cristina grabbed me tightly, holding me close to the bars. Saving me from any harm.

Ben yelled out, "We have you! We have you!"

Catching my breath, I grabbed onto the bars and lowered myself down safely with their help.

With a sense of relief, I looked at both of them face-to-face, "Thank you."

Determined, I turned around and faced the gauntlet of wind, falling down in its gale.

Ben shouted to me, "This wind is worse than before! You are not strong enough to withstand this storm! We can find another way."

I turned back to them and responded with utmost urgency, "STAND BY TO CRAWL UNDER THE GATE!" I headed down the passageway. I kept low and turned my head to the side to reduce the amount of wind and dust hitting me in the face.

When I returned to the Cryptex, I grabbed the other end of the cable and pulled it near the edge of the cylinder and made another loop. I picked up the pole and wedged it between the stairs and broke it in half. I inserted one portion into the Cryptex hole and attached the loop to it. As the Cryptex slowly rotated, the rope became tighter.

Cristina's notes were no longer in my possession. I had to remember the details of what the three of us discussed earlier. With the other half of the broken pole, I walked up the stairway, almost getting blown off by the increasing winds. I inserted the pole into the second rune level hole. I started pushing the pole to rotate the layer, but my leverage now on the shortened pole had changed, making it very difficult to rotate. Slowly, the segment started to turn. I aligned the rune with the next letter: E.

Panels on the second rune layers opened up and the winds picked up. I pulled out the pole and continued up the stairs. The Cryptex was still slowly rotating and, hopefully, also pulling the gate up for Cristina and Ben to escape. I could hear the cable making stretching noises as it became more taut. I hoped the cable was strong enough for just a few more minutes.

I inserted the pole into the third level and struggled to rotate the proper rune toward the proper letter: L. Click. Another layer done. One more to go. Another set of panels opened up and the winds increased, knocking me over the edge of the stairs.

I hung on to the stair step with my right hand and my legs flailing below. I reached up with my left hand and tried to connect with the stair, but my hand slipped. I could probably fall to the ground, but would likely break both legs or something else and would tragically end this night's farcical adventure — and, we would all die.

I couldn't hang on for much more. I tried to swing forward and latch my leg onto something. My fingers were starting to cramp up. I could feel myself slipping away — when something from above grabbed my hand.

Ben yelled out, "I HAVE YOU! Give us your other hand." I lifted my left hand and Cristina grabbed hold. They pulled me up to the stairs. To safety. The cable had lifted the gate enough for them to escape.

Cristina pulled the pole from the last segment and inserted it into the fourth and last level. Both of them pushed the pole forward, aligning the rune to the letter: O. Before the wind panels opened up, Ben pulled me up and we rose to the top of the Cryptex.

At the cylinder's apex, the three of us positioned ourselves around a tabletop-like structure with a rope centered in the middle shooting straight up.

Cristina held on to the lantern with its flame struggling to stay lit. Either way, the fuel was out.

The winds howled around us. Ben yelled, "What do we do from here?" There was another puzzle that needed to be solved. We stopped asking if this was the last one.

I looked at the table closely, examining every feature. The table contained three sets of three discs, nine discs total, with six random letters on each disc. Centered within each of the three disc sets was a button that had three etched lines pointing to each of the discs. Each center disc had the Roman numerals: I, II, III. What did these numerals mean and what did the letters on the discs signify?

Confused and emotionally distraught, Cristina spoke up, "This does not make any sense. No sense at all!"

Ben was equally distressed. "This whole escapade was for what? To teach us something? To protect some valuables?"

I tried to retain my composure but was physically slipping fast. "I don't know why he did this. I only know that we can't give up now. There IS a way!"

Cristina started crying and replied with deep despair, "This day was supposed to be a great day. And look where it ended."

At that moment, I remembered how Leonardo began each and every day. Could that be it? I offered my only idea, "I think this day might be a successful day."

The others looked at me with equal confusion.

"Do you remember how Leonardo has us start and end each day with the phrase, *Agite*

Excelsius?" I looked down at the table. "Maybe that phrase is our answer out of here."

I was at numeral "I" position and looked at the discs in front of me. Spelling out *Agite* did not work for the discs in my position or either of the other two disc sets.

I counted on my fingers and spelled out in my mind. "YES! *Excelsius*. Nine letters! Nine discs! *Excelsius!*"

I spelled out my three letters: "E-X-C."

Cristina spelled out hers: "E-L-S."

Ben spelled out his: "I-U-S."

Nothing happened. What was supposed to happen? What did the three center discs with Roman numerals do?

I yelled out, "I got it! I think we need to tell the Cryptex to unlock itself. We just entered the combination."

Ben pressed down on his center disc. It didn't press down. I tried mine and Cristina tried hers. Nothing. We tried rotating the disc. Nothing.

At the center of the disc was a tiny slot, just larger than a fingernail. Ben inserted his thumbnail and tried to turn it, but his nail split. We needed something stronger. The winds were hitting us from all directions. We needed a break and some luck. That was when I reached deep into my pocket and pulled out three coins. Three lucky coins. I handed one each to Ben and Cristina. We inserted them into the slot and turned the discs. "On my count, press your center disc. ONE! TWO! THREE! NOW!"

We all pressed our disc at the same time. The panels in the Cryptex closed and the winds stopped immediately.

We looked at each other, waiting for something to happen. The Cryptex platform and entire structure started to rumble. I yelled again, "Hold onto each other's hands. NOW!" We leaned in and held hands as tightly as we could.

The platform started to rise away from the cylindrical outer structure. Upward, faster and faster, rising with the rope at the center. The force of the wind provided lift beneath us, sending the entire platform higher. Toward where, I wasn't sure. The secret released within this Cryptex elevated us upwards — and we were the passengers.

The entire structure shook and wobbled. "HOLD ON! DON'T LET GO!"

The wooden boards below me loosened and then broke off. I repositioned my foot onto another board.

Then some boards below Cristina came loose and she slipped from our handhold — screamed. Ben and I held her hands tightly. How long would this ride last before the whole thing broke apart?

Fifteen-seconds passed with the entire elevator shaking wildly. And as quickly as it started, the platform stopped. We looked at each other in confusion and welcomed relief.

Surrounding us now were four walls. We could barely move around; the walls were tight to the platform. Was this another puzzle? We were now in a very small room, if you could call it that.

Ben yelled, "When will this end!" At least we weren't moving at breakneck speeds or being challenged by the wind or anything else. But what was next?

The flame from the lantern barely illuminated the room. Ben noticed that three walls had the same wood pattern, with the planks arranged in the same direction. On the wall behind me, the planks looked different.

I slowly turned my body around in our tight quarters. I felt a large knot extruding from the wood. Not a knot. It was a doorknob. This side was not only a wall, but it had a door. I pushed the knob as hard as I could, with my back positioned against the platform's table. Nothing.

I tried again and the door opened, and this time I fell to the ground. Ben and Cristina followed me out. The door was not simply a door; it was the "Exit" door immediately outside of Leonardo's studio.

CHAPTER 17 - CONSEQUENCES

I was facedown, nose to the floor, when I felt water dripping on my head. I looked up and saw Leonardo — wet, drenched, and with a forbidding look on his face. His beard and clothes were soaked. And Giovanna and Lorenzo stood right next to him.

Leonardo spoke up, "The sun has just risen. And so should you." Ben and Cristina helped me to stand up.

With dark clouds retreating to the west, the morning light shone through the window in the hallway. We were at Leonardo's studio door, three dirty, exhausted, and guilty associates.

Leonardo looked directly into my eyes, "I just returned to the studio. I postponed my trip because heavy rains flooded the roads and bridges leading out of town. And this young woman here, Giovanna, greeted me in my return. She told me that she went to help someone feed the chickens this morning but that this person wasn't there. And upon further inspection, the person had not returned home that evening or at all. For some reason, Giovanna thought to come back here, to my studio, to hope and find you, Francesco. It seems like she was right and that you had two others to keep you company."

Leonardo patted Lorenzo on the back. "I had planned for Lorenzo to watch over the studio. He was familiar with the layout down there since he helped repair and renovate many sections years ago. When he saw you enter the labyrinth, he followed you to make sure you were okay down there. I told him explicitly to not help you out. That you three must work together."

Lorenzo looked at us three in a cheerful manner. "Hey, looks like you made it just fine. Good to see the three of you again."

We smiled at Lorenzo and then over to Leonardo with sorrowful dispositions. I spoke first, "Yes, sir. I tried to sneak into the studio last night to see the secrets you were hiding."

Ben and Cristina answered in unison, "Me too."

Leonardo continued, but he did not seem overly upset, "I see you have experienced my labyrinth of hell. I call it my *Codex Silenda*. It was intended for thieves and crooks, not apprentices. What you did, or tried to do, was cheating. You disobeyed a direct order. A great man once said, 'I would prefer even to fail with honor than win by cheating.' I hope you learned your lesson."

Cristina replied with great remorse, "Yes, sir. We did."

Ben added, "We are sorry, sir. It will not happen again."

Leonardo looked at the three of us with deep reservation, "What disturbs me more were your earlier disagreements with each other, where you took sides on something that the other had a passion for. Never disrespect someone else's ideas or passion. Never. To be great, you have to show respect and humility."

We all nodded our heads in agreement. Had what Leonardo told us that early morning, after that long night, been life lessons that addressed our fundamental existence?

He continued, "You will not know everything. So, you must trust in others, and learn from others. Poor is the pupil who does not surpass his master. I teach you to know what I know. It is up to you to reach beyond and fulfill your own potential. Then you will become the Master. Are there any questions?"

There were so many things going through my mind, including the lifelessness in my foot. But I asked him, "This labyrinth beneath us, where did it come from?"

"This building was built upon an old wine cellar. I had devised an ingenious transport device to retrieve crates of wine from all areas below. A specially designed windmill on top of the house powers its movement and many other mechanisms below. Sometimes it seems like these devices have a mind of their own. The transport was very useful as some of the passageways got too windy from the various outside vents and drainage grates, creating a powerful vortex. I didn't want to go down there anymore. It always pitched dust in my eyes and messed up my hair."

I shrugged my shoulder, shook my head, and solemnly responded, "I don't think your transport device works anymore, sir."

Leonardo sighed, "Hmm, that is too bad."

I didn't have any regrets smashing that device to pieces. In retrospect, I kind of enjoyed it.

Leonardo continued, "Before the cellar, it was an underground cavern, carved by water and time. Several years ago, I had the entire complex fashioned into what you see now. A security system and puzzles of sorts to protect my investments. I have not had time to keep up with its maintenance and some areas have gone into disrepair. How would you rate the obstacles?"

Ben quickly responded, "Very difficult, sir."

Cristina replied, "And definitely challenging."

I added, "I don't plan on going through that again."

Leonardo gave out a loud laugh. The three of us were definitely tired and physically exhausted, and I was in considerable pain, but we joined Leonardo in his laughter.

Leonardo noticed, "You all look a bit famished. Did you not drink or eat the apples I left?"

Cristina added, "The apples were rotten and the wine bottle was broken. So no, we did not eat at all."

"Hmm, that's strange. I thought I checked on that before I left town. Sorry about that. And remind me later to tell you about the stairs. It is much easier to get back up here."

Leonardo placed both hands on Giovanna's shoulders. "Ahem, onto more positive notes. I would like to introduce you to my new apprentice. While we waited for you three to take flight and escape the labyrinth below, Giovanna explained her passion as a bird puppeteer, which equals my deep interest in birds and their flight. She will work with me in my organization and development of my next codices[39] on birds. That is, Francesco, if you don't think you'll get distracted working in the same studio together."

Although now in tremendous pain, I grimaced, "That is okay with me, sir."

Leonardo looked at me and my foot, "But first, before we all go home and get a good rest, let's go into the studio and check on Francesco's injury. Plus, I have some water and fruit."

I winced once more, "Thank you, sir. Anything you can do to help."

---

[39] Codices → Notebook pages; manuscript text in book form.

Leonardo pulled out two keys and inserted them each into the door's locks. Reminiscent of an earlier time last night, the three of us apprentices stepped back a few paces, clearing our footing on the iris.

Leonardo turned around and laughed, "What, you don't trust my keys?" He slowly turned one lock and then the next. Each lock provided its reassuring click. Leonardo opened the door and we all breathed a sigh of relief.

The day after our near-disastrous escapade, I rested and recuperated peacefully in bed until late afternoon. My foot was wrapped up and raised high above a pile of pillows. Giovanna, Cristina, and Ben came over and offered their support and encouragement. I realized each one of them had become even closer friends. Though Giovanna had no idea of the adventure we experienced in the caverns, she started to comprehend the excitement and dangers we overcame. I explained to her the whole story and, though she was glad that I didn't kill myself, she was happier that she didn't need to trudge through the dirty, wet, and dark caverns in the middle of the night.

My parents didn't know the full story of my misadventures in Leonardo's cave of mystery and deception. All they knew was that I was out late at night with my friends and that I hurt my foot. That was good enough for me.

Over the course of the next week, Giovanna, Cristina, and Ben joined me each day at home. Giovanna arrived at my house before dawn and assisted Niccolo in feeding the chickens. Momma made my favorite meals and delivered them right to my room.

Everyone helped in my painful convalescence. Ben supported me moving around the house, while Cristina pampered me with pillows to rest my foot. They all offered me kind bedside manners. Giovanna was a great help and probably didn't mind seeing me more often now than when I started the apprenticeship.

I wasn't used to staying indoors for longer than a day, so after a few days being cooped up, I turned restless, itching for some fresh air. The crutches Leonardo gave me worked out well as they allowed me to walk without putting pressure on my bad foot. I wore a sock on my foot to keep my toes warm.

My friends and I walked around my house and around the neighborhood, and talked about our lives and our future together. Having time together gave me a better appreciation for each of them.

Since Ben, Cristina, and I would need to resume our apprentice duties with Leonardo, the four of us, now including Giovanna, decided to meet every Saturday morning in town to catch up on everything.

CHAPTER 18 - SPECTRA

We returned to Leonardo's studio at the end of the week. I sat in the corner of the workshop and looked out the window. Our town's apothecary provided Laudanum[40] medicine to help ease the pain in my foot. I remember feeling much better, but I sometimes hallucinated or felt lightheaded. Not the worst feeling I've had, but one I didn't want to continue.

I tried to concentrate on my architectural drawings, but my mind was elsewhere. Cristina worked on a clay sculpture and Ben continued on a painting that Leonardo had started.

Ben asked Leonardo, "Sir, what happened with the crates and other things that were here in the studio?" Overhearing Ben's question and also equally curious, Cristina and I refocused our attention to hear Leonardo's response.

---

[40] <u>Laudanum</u> → An opium-based painkiller.

"They were picked up yesterday under armed guard and are on their way to Paris. The contents of which are still secret. If the contents of those boxes were to fall into the wrong hands, they would have devastating and calamitous consequences. These are what wars are fought over."

Reacting to Leonardo's response, Ben lost focus and dropped one of his paint brushes on the floor. Leonardo walked over and picked up the brush and placed it on the table. "Here Ben, you'll need to wash that up. Don't use this dirty brush on the canvas. And no, I'm not going to tell you. A secret is a secret." He gazed at each of us and continued with a smile, "I think one adventure is enough for the three of you for the time being."

Leonardo walked over to me and asked how I was feeling. I looked up at him, "Fine, sir. Much better. These crutches are very useful."

He talked to me for a few minutes about human and animal body structures, specifically the various and many bones and muscles in the foot and leg. He pulled out a few anatomical sketches he had done recently. I winced every time I shifted positions to get a better glimpse.

He saw that I had trouble maintaining my attention for more than a few seconds, and asked, "Your focus in out of focus. Get up and follow me."

I grabbed my crutches and followed Leonardo to the back room — his secret room.

He slowly opened the door. "Now, take off your shoe."

I slipped my shoe off my good foot.

Leonardo helped me walk into the room. As I entered, my heartbeat increased with anticipation on seeing this private room, held *sub rosa* from us apprentices for months.

I looked up as Leonardo reached for the door handle. Cristina and Ben looked at me in disbelief and surprise — and excitement. I smiled at them as the door closed. I finally made it into Leonardo's secret escape, his private lair.

I looked up and saw the room was illuminated with light from the ceiling. One of the glass domes I had noticed earlier from outside was a glass window in the ceiling.

Surrounding me were four walls and the floor that were affixed with opalescent sequins distributed around pieces of iridescent glass and mirrors. Integrated between the pieces were splashes of color painted with the rainbow hues of white, gray, red, orange, yellow, green, blue, magenta, rose, pink, slate, olive, brown, and black. The entire floor was smooth and polished like a calm summer lake at dawn. Positioned in front of me was a simple rocking chair at the center of the room.

Leonardo explained, "This room is special place where I get to be alone. I named it *Spectra*. It provides me a place with little distraction, for me to clear my mind and ... think."

I thought there was more to it. Though the room was colorful and unique, it didn't provide me with any special inspiration. It was nice. Maybe the drugs dulled my senses. I didn't think so.

He continued, "The dome on the east side of the studio roof gets the first sunshine of the day. In the second dome on the west side, at a certain time of day when the sun is overhead for a period of about ninety minutes, a spectacle of light enters from above."

I looked overhead and noticed a structure of several prisms, connected together.

"What you see above you is a dodecagonal[41] with transparent prismatic honeycomb sides. It is a complex prism, where I have constructed a kaleidoscope-like device with mirrors and other refracting surfaces. All made near Venezia with faceted clear Murano glass triedri prisms[42]."

I complimented him on his creation, "This is a magnificent looking structure. It is very abstract, unique, and beautiful."

Leonardo walked beneath the window and clarified my statement, "Ah, Francesco, the structure is more than that. This is a vehicle that transforms the abundance of traveling light. I have split the light into two paths. One path channels the sun's light through a tubular tunnel down into the caverns below. The other directs light into this room. When the sun hits the skylight at a certain time of day, my mind is able to relax and think."

Leonardo turned to me and changed to a serious face, "Cristina and Ben explained to me that you were the one who kept his wits about him down there. That is a mark of a true hero and a gifted artist."

---

[41] <u>Dodecagonal</u> → A twelve-sided shape.
[42] <u>Triedri prisms</u> → Long triangular glass rod crystals.

I disputed his declaration, "I am not a hero and I am not an artist or an architect. I am learning from you everything to make me become better."

"Down there, you were a true artist who, at great odds, and with everything to lose, pulled together all your physical and mental resources. You endured your injury with great fortitude, functioned under great pressure, and rationalized an escape. That is to be commended."

"Thank you. I have two questions that have been puzzling me. Why did you only provide us with a map? You could have left tools or instructions for us."

"But I did leave you tools; three of them. They were the best tools to free you from everything you encountered. They were Cristina, Ben, and Francesco. I left it up to the three of you: to analyze, to evaluate, to interpret, to think critically, to reason, and to work together as a team. You did not need a map. You had everything you needed, less some drink and apples." He shared another one of his "if-you-have-to-ask-you-already-know-the-answer" grins and smiled brightly.

He was right. Absolutely right. We challenged the depths of the labyrinth with our minds. That was all we needed.

"And what was your other question?"

"Could you please explain how the intricate apparatuses and mechanisms for Codex Silenda were created? How long did it take to build? Did anyone help you?" I had many more questions to ask him about the Codex but decided to start out simple.

"Francesco, in due time, you will know all that you need to know about Codex Silenda, and then improve upon it. I had sketches and drawings, but they were destroyed in a fire a couple of years ago. Nothing exists now."

Still dazed from the pain and probably a bit from the medication, Leonardo helped me sit down in the chair. I leaned back and stretched my legs. Wincing more now, the pain was starting to come back and my head was slowly turning in circles.

Leonardo continued, "You are my star apprentice. In addition to your regular assignments and duties, I have a special project for you: build a model, a miniature Codex Silenda replica representing the challenges you all went through down there. But on a smaller scale.

Something a child or budding artist could use, learn from, and be inspired by."

He further explained, "But there is one rule you must follow: when adapting this model, transform the challenges and solutions of the real maze so that would-be thieves are not provided the answers through the child's puzzle."

He repeated his familiar phrase, "Remember that simplicity is the ultimate sophistication. But first: Dream, Design, Sketch, Create."

This time, I acknowledged his directive, "Yes, sir. I will protect your secret."

Before Leonardo left the room, he offered me some creative support, "Francesco, think about this next assignment. Remember the details of your adventure below this studio. Stay in here for a bit, relax, and see if you can create magnificence." He turned and exited the room. How was I going to transform and create the complexity of Codex Silenda?

I repositioned myself in the chair and took a breath of air. The chair had two bands of walnut wood that curved around to form the rockers. The long arms were scooped out in the center to provide a place to cradle my arms. Thin, curved, and flexible wooden splats of chestnut formed the back. The chair was very relaxing and comfortably supported my entire frame, head, arms, and legs.

I leaned back and saw fragments of the beautiful blue sky. Then a large cloud moved away from the sun and enabled a ray of light to penetrate through the skylight.

At that moment, Spectra, Leonardo's colorful menagerie creation, communicated its beauty. The circular dome allowed the light to strike the kaleidoscope and reflect into the dodecagonal prisms. Then downward into the moving cluster of individual prisms.

All at once, the entire room was filled with a spectrum of color that was diffused and dispersed around my head. With the light bouncing off the walls, the floors, and enhancing all my senses, this dancing rainbow of beauty, in its incredible simplicity and subtle complexity, calmed my pain and anxiety. I felt a strange ethereal glow softly warm my entire body. I no longer sensed discomfort in my foot or any other part of my body.

My heartbeat slowed and I felt each beat resonate through my body. I closed my eyes every few seconds to fully absorb the serene state of being I was experiencing. I am not sure if I was fully conscious or unconscious during the encounter, going in and out of a dream-like state. I felt tranquil and relaxed, and had the strange feeling of weightlessness, floating above the room, free of any physical restrictions.

I am not sure how long this feeling lasted as time didn't matter. I was mesmerized, enchanted, and inspired through the playful escapade of light. I started to think about Leonardo's Codex Silenda assignment. I imagined a simple structured book made out of wood with five pages of intricate puzzles. Each page featuring a unique challenge that required the reader to solve each page's puzzle to unlock the next page, which was epic and truly inspirational.

I must have dozed off because when I awoke, I remembered dreaming a mindblowing adventure through the labyrinth of mazes and challenges within Codex Silenda; every underground passageway, obstacle, and solution was vividly etched in my memory.

Looking up at the skylight, the sun no longer provided its rays for inspiration. The spectacular colors in the room were no more; that was — until tomorrow. But this session or wild daydream was over. The innovative seeds of creativity were successfully planted in my mind. This puzzle book was going to be legendary. Created by me, Francesco Aiello of Florence, apprentice to the great master, Leonardo di ser Piero da Vinci.

I exited the room where Ben and Cristina were done cleaning up from their day's activities. I shared smiles with each of them. I saw the familiar signals, the rub of the nose and the pull of an ear, and I returned with a wipe of my brow. It was our newly created secret signal we gave each other to remind us to get together on Saturday morning.

The next morning, for our first meetup, Niccolo and Serena kindly relieved me of my chicken feeding and cleaning duties, which I gracefully accepted — though it was probably only for a limited time while I was recovering.

Giovanna met me at our front door and, with crutches in hand, we headed down to the Palazzo della Signoria. We met up with Ben and Cristina in the town square and had a great time talking, relaxing, and enjoying each other's company.

We shared stories about what we would do after our apprenticeship: our goals and ambitions for our future, my life with Giovanna. We even developed a special four-way handshake as a sign of loyalty to each other. Our perspectives had changed, or rather matured, since that first day in the studio.

Some of our best memories were from these get-togethers. When it rained on the weekends, we still got together but convened at my house as Momma provided tasty foods to keep us energized with our favorite snacks, cheeses, and *charcuterie*[43].

Momma never complained about our odd hours, which ran late into the night. We never complained either and thanked her profusely.

---

[43] Charcuterie → Prepared meat products that are salted or cured, such as bacon, ham, and sausage.

EPILOGUE: KODA KHRONIKA

Over the course of the year, Cristina, Ben, and I worked on several projects for customers who had commissioned distinctive works by Leonardo. Many of his clients included monarchs and dukes, churches and monasteries, all who offered large-scale commissions for his works. These items included mostly paintings, altarpieces, and sculptures.

Other projects took us to remote cities where the actual work had to be performed — paintings of walls, ceilings, and frescoes. For these completed projects, Leonardo often had one of us travel with him to deliver these pieces.

We traveled on multi-week trips across the countryside to make these deliveries. Destinations included Murano, to survey its colorful, elaborate, and skillfully made artistic glass, and Venezia, to traverse its wonderfully intricate canals, both cities built on water; Milan to explore the famous metalworks that included spectacular suits of armor; Bologna to experience its social and cultural life surrounded by its towers and lengthy porticoes; Cesena to enrich our minds and probe the large volume of books, codices, and manuscripts in its *Biblioteca Malatestiana*[44], and of

---

[44] *Biblioteca Malatestiana* → Malatestiana Library (Italian: Biblioteca Malatestiana), also known as the Malatesta Novello Library, is a public library in the city of Cesena in northern Italy.

course, to taste its wonderful wines; and to Roma to stroll its architectural monuments and absorb its Papal presence.

These excursions gave Leonardo a chance to personally deliver the masterpieces to his clients and to further negotiate new works in the process. During these trips on the road, he often shared his visions of mechanic water devices, weaponry concepts, and scientific and human anatomical discoveries from dissecting a human body — from a deceased person, of course! These tours enriched my technical and scientific understanding of the limitless possibilities playing within Leonardo's world, and broadened my perspectives of artistry, culture, knowledge, and architecture.

When I was back in the studio, during my spare time or after work at home, I worked on the Codex Silenda assignment Leonardo had given me. I spent this extra time sketching several designs for the overall layout of the puzzle.

Giovanna fashioned draft concepts for the pulleys and gears. Cristina helped me cut and shape the panels of wood and all of its inter-connected functional pieces for each of the five pages. Ben provided his painting and staining skills for all the parts that made the overall presentation of the puzzle more visibly alluring. Working together, we all shared our unique skills and passion that created a beautiful work of art.

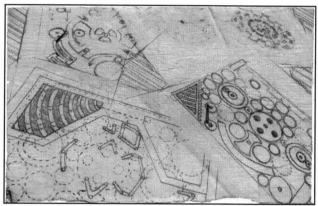

Leonardo checked our progress throughout the process. But since the inner workings of the Codex Silenda book were "secret," I tried to hide the project from his view. I told him, "This work is very important and it is not ready to be revealed ... yet." I smiled and shooed him on his way. He would not give up.

If you were Leonardo da Vinci, how would you curb someone's desire to discover a secret? Hmm. Unfortunately, I did not have a secret labyrinth.

At the end of the year, we finished five Codex Silenda puzzles. The amount of detail that went into puzzle was daunting, hundreds of individual pieces that included springs, gears, wheels, bolts, pegs, and boards. All the components sanded, wood-burned or etched, and painted or stained. And each of the five intricate puzzle segments perfectly assembled and coupled into the Codex Silenda puzzle.

We each provided our signatures to each of the puzzles. Leonardo provided a special message on each as a remembrance of our time as apprentices with him. Of course, on each puzzle he wrote the familiar phrase from our daily charge, *Agite Excelsius!*

On the day of our parting, one year to the day we stepped foot in the studio, Leonardo had each of us scribe our last journal post on a separate piece of paper, an insight into our experience and wisdom gained, and gift a token of ourselves, which were all placed neatly alongside the puzzle book, which itself was encased in its very own puzzle casing.

I carried it in a procession with Leonardo, Ben, and Cristina, down into the recesses of Codex Silenda labyrinth, to be entombed as a capsule of our times together. Returning to his studio, Leonardo talked about a new concept, the ornithopter, a device that would allow humans to soar through the air like birds. As always, I was fascinated with everything he talked about.

I was reminded of something he once told us, "Learning never exhausts the mind." Leonardo embodied that spirit with his inventive imagination and unquenchable curiosity.

Then Leonardo bundled up some scrolls and picked up some pencils. It looked like the Master was going to work more at home — a man with ten thousand ideas. But first, our farewell dinner courtesy of Momma.

I expressed another smile of satisfaction and gratitude to be one of his apprentices, and a friend. Leonardo glanced in my direction, looking directly into my eyes, and then proceeded toward the door. Had he just shown the faintest hint of a smile? The Master? He sure did.

Ben, Cristina, Giovanna, and I approached the door to leave and celebrated in unison one last time, "*Agite Excelsius!*"

A grand dinner was the perfect finale to our year-long adventure. Momma insisted we celebrate the end of our apprenticeship with a fabulous meal with friends and their families. Ben's family, Cristina's mother, Giovanna's family, and Leonardo da Vinci were all invited, even Lorenzo. We were to get together later that afternoon at my house. But before our big event, I needed to change — in a way that was new for me.

Throughout this last year as an apprentice, having been given more responsibilities by Leonardo, and with my changes in relationship to Giovanna and my friends, I felt older and more mature, with a more grown-up outlook on life. Maybe it was just me, but this inner change needed an outer refinement that reflected and complemented this outlook.

After getting home from the studio and with the help of Niccolo holding a mirror, in secret I cut and styled my long hair. I had not realized how much effort it was to manage my appearance every morning. I don't know if Giovanna or Momma would approve, but that was okay because I approved. Either way, it was too late. The task was done. I put on my best clean clothes for the evening.

With Niccolo following behind grinning from ear-to-ear, I slowly stepped downstairs to see Momma in the kitchen and surprise her. As I turned around the corner, she glanced at me while arranging the cheeses on the plate. She took a second look and offered in a curious tone. "What have we here?" With her hands full of cheese slices, she gave me a gleaming white smile and waved for me to come to her.

I walked into the kitchen next to her with a small grin on my face. "Hi, Momma."

She looked back at me. "I see you've cleaned yourself up very nicely. Looks like you are ready for something important. How about … helping set the tables outside? People are starting to arrive and there's a lot more to get ready." Niccolo giggled.

"Okay, Momma."

"And by the way, you look so handsome."
With a tear in her eye, she leaned over and
gave me a kiss on the cheek.

"Thanks, Momma. You're the best."

"Niccolo, now you help your brother set
up. Outside for the both of you. There's much
to do in here."

I was happy that Momma approved. Not
that she needed to, but I felt much better.

Niccolo and I went outside and helped set
up the tables end-to-end, move the chairs, and
place the table decorations. This was still an
informal gathering, but dressed up a bit.

Cristina and her Momma arrived, as did
Ben and Giovanna and their families, and
finally Leonardo. The women headed into the
house while the rest of us finished setting up.
The smells from inside the house lingered in
the air. What a wonderful aroma of flavors and
spices.

This was our graduation celebration. A
special meal for a special occasion. I felt
melancholy that our time together as
apprentices, as friends, would take different
paths. Paths we had dreamed about, but career
paths different from each other's. This dinner
was an opportunity to say *arrivederci*[45].

Cristina and Ben walked up to me. Cristina gave me a soft nudge on my shoulders. "Hey Francesco, you look different from earlier today. Nice."

Ben poked my other shoulder and offered his astute observation with a sly grin, "Nice, man! You clean up real nice ... almost as nice as ... Benvenuto."

Giovanna walked up behind me, turned me around, and gave me a kiss on the lips. She ran her hands through my shortened hair. "He's all mine, apprentices, all mine," she whispered into my ear. "... And don't change anything else. You look fantastic."

My skin immediately warmed up and my face turned red. "I must have walked in the sun way too much today ... or something like that." The whole group laughed. I think my makeover went as well as could be expected.

Leonardo walked up to our group. "Hello, my fellow apprentices. I am so glad you invited me to this special event. The appetizing aromas that waft through the air are preparing my palate for a sumptuous evening." Leonardo handed me a box of apples and jugs of water.

---

[45] <u>Arrivederci</u> → A farewell remark. Goodbye. An acknowledgment or expression of goodwill at parting.

"And don't say that I didn't reserve fresh apples and cold water for my friends. Just don't let them go bad in your cellar ... or underground caverns, if you have any. Eat them and enjoy a drink on me."

The group chuckled and thanked him for his generosity. We followed Leonardo around the yard and introduced him to our families.

For it was Leonardo who brought us together and moved us toward an exciting path and future. The warm air of the afternoon was beginning to cool, making our special gathering very enjoyable.

Serena came out of the house and pleasantly, in a very ladylike manner, called our dinner to order, "*La cena è pronta, mangiamo!*[46]" The families and Leonardo sat around the long table. The mothers brought out the first course, an antipasto of prosciutto and cheeses, bruschetta, and salmon. While we started eating, Ben and Cristina joked at the games they used to play while waiting for Leonardo to wake up during *riposo*, like placing a parade of miniature clay sculptures of animals around the

---

[46] *La cena è pronta, mangiamo* → Dinner is ready. Let's eat.

edge of his desk. Leonardo grinned and shared a laugh with us.

During the next course, fish soup and the sautéed gnocchi alla fungi with fresh mushrooms that Serena and Niccolo picked from the garden, Leonardo explained a new method for harvesting mushrooms which could, theoretically, harvest a bushel every minute using his mechanical plucking device. Serena's eyes were wide open. "So I don't need to get my hands dirty anymore?" The whole table laughed and we complimented her on the fine job she and Niccolo had done.

I looked around the table as we finished off the soup. Our meal had just started and I felt that my larger family of close friends had been with me my whole life. It amazed me that these friendships were just waiting to be formed and all I needed to do was to take that first step and say, "Hello."

Momma brought out her signature lamb roast with green beans and herb roasted potatoes. And later, a fresh garden salad with crushed pistachios sprinkled on top. Celebrating with good food, good friends, and good times — this was true happiness.

Ben shared with us what he usually did at the end of the work week. "Most weekends, I headed back to the farm and helped my family. I shared all my earnings with them. My brothers and I did odd jobs around the farm, and general upkeep on the barn and house." He laughed and added, "And replaced fence posts so the cattle did not escape and visit me in Florence."

Ben said that because of his apprenticeship, all his brothers now took art lessons from him to learn how to paint. And to capture the spirit of the painting, Ben shared the story that Leonardo had told the apprentices: to close their eyes and imagine a bird flying over a lake set against tall majestic mountains on a beautiful blue sky day. "My brothers are on their way to becoming great artists. As long as they don't draw on our neighbor's houses." Ben had become the teacher.

Cristina shared with us how last summer, Ben, Giovanna, and I showed her how to swim at our local pond. "Swimming was never at the top of my list of things I needed to learn. It wasn't that I was afraid of water. I didn't find time until recently."

Cristina mentioned that when she and her mother needed help after her Papa died, the church and neighbors were there for them. When she wanted to learn to swim, it was her friends who came to the rescue. "There are good people everywhere I go and I learned not to be afraid to reach out and ask. Life is certainly better with good friends."

Hearing Ben and Cristina share their inner thoughts reinforced within me that each of our lives is unique and special, and should never be taken for granted. Each of us have something to offer one another.

It was my turn to offer my thoughts. "When I started my apprenticeship one year ago, Leonardo da Vinci charged me to challenge myself, to create from my heart, to always be learning, and to apply what I've learned. And if I didn't reach out to others, then my education and experiences, and the love for what I enjoy doing most, would be lost forever. I needed to share my world with others.

"Cristina, Ben, Giovanna, and Leonardo, family isn't always blood. It's the people in your life who want you in theirs, the ones who accept you for who you are. The ones who would do anything to see you smile and who love you no matter what."

There was a long pause after I spoke. Not an uncomfortable one, but one where we each had a chance to absorb what each other said and reflect on those special sentiments. Happiness was sitting around this table and I didn't want the moment to end.

The mothers left the table and went into the house. For Momma, she knew that after tonight, we would all be going our separate ways, finding our next calling. My chair at the dinner table would be empty while I was on that new adventure — and maybe not returning. I was the first in the family to move out and move on as an adult. That left me thinking about what I would miss the most.

The women returned with the most important items of the night: *dolce*[47], cannoli dipped in chocolate, fresh fruit, and hot tea. I would miss her cooking and desserts. I'd definitely return back home often for a home-cooked meal — and of course to give my family a great, big hug.

As we finished our dessert, Ben stood up and tapped his fork on his tea cup. He looked

---

[47] <u>Dolce</u> → A sweet; dessert.

me right in the eye. The gathering became quiet. "Francesco, do you remember in the Codex Silenda labyrinth when I called out 'You're not strong enough to withstand the storm'? Well, I was wrong. You proved me wrong. You were the storm. And have been a wonderful inspiration for us this last year."

The entire table erupted in applause. I sat back and smiled ever so brightly. It sunk in, *I was the storm!*

I stood up and cleared my throat. "Thank you, Ben. When I started in this studio, I was a young man trying to figure out who I was and where I was headed in life. My friends gave me support. Leonardo da Vinci gave me discipline and structure. But my parents gave me encouragement, perseverance, and strength — to never quit and to try new things."

Momma and Papa stood up and gave me a big hug. Momma squeezed my cheeks. "Francesco, you have always been self-motivated and talented. We tried to encourage your interests and celebrate your successes, and we wanted you to pursue your heart's desires. You are a good and honest boy."

"Thanks, Momma. But I should have told you this before. When I hurt my foot months ago, it is because I had disobeyed Leonardo and snuck into his studio. And then strayed into dark, dangerous, and unforgiving underground caverns as a result. That's the Codex Silenda that Ben just mentioned." I kissed Momma on her cheek and whispered in her ear, "Sorry, Momma."

I turned toward Ben and Cristina. "When I was at that last challenge, the Cryptex, and the winds were blowing in my face and my foot was in immense pain, all I thought of were you two. Not only talented artists, but my dear friends. I would do anything for you. The task ahead of me was never greater than the strength that was within me. My strength did not come from my physical capacity; it came from my indomitable will and love for you. And it was there all the time inside of me, keeping me company."

Cristina and Ben got out of their chairs and joined together in a friendship hug. The three of us together for the last time. As Cristina started to cry, we couldn't let her tear up alone, so Ben and I joined her.

Leonardo tapped his glass three times with his fork. The three of us turned toward him and wiped our tears away. He stood up, raised his glass, and called us by name. "Cristina Rosso, Benvenuto Farnese, Giovanna Bronzino, and Francesco Aiello, these last twelve months have flown by quickly. This was a valuable time for me to share my knowledge and experience with the four of you. YOU provided the creativity. Our time here as artists is precious. My legacy is now shared with four special and talented people."

We all looked at each other and gleamed with a sense of accomplishment and great achievement.

"But as apprentices, one year was all you were offered. Except, there was a test of mine that you did not expect; it was the Codex Silenda. You were the first apprentices to experience this labyrinth. And you passed. You showed endurance, resilience, and physical, mental, and emotional strength that enabled courage in the face of adversity. It is that, combined with the diverse suite of artistic talents each of you have shown me over this last year, that takes each of you beyond and onto a different plane of creative, imaginative, inventive, and expressive possibilities."

We all looked at each other a bit confused. What was Leonardo saying? A test?

217

"I fully understand if you wish to take off into your own directions. You are all fully qualified and will make our town, or wherever you go, very proud. But I would be honored to have you continue as my Master Apprentices for a few more years." He paused for a moment and looked straight into our eyes.

From the very beginning at that first interview, Leonardo knew what we were capable of. He believed in us. He didn't treat us like children, but challenged us to strive to do our very best. He knew our potential even when we questioned our own abilities. He always gave credit where it was due. Though Leonardo was the Master, he was a gentle and caring teacher who established a workplace for us to learn. Without question.

Ben, Cristina, Giovanna, and I looked at each other and knew where our next steps would be. A genuine happiness together with our Master. We each reached for our glasses and raised them high into the air, one at a time.

Cristina spoke first, "*Agite Excelsius.*"

Then Ben, "*Agite Excelsius.*"

Then Giovanna, "*Agite Excelsius!*"

Then me, "*Agite Excelsius!!*"

Leonardo was choked up. His eyes glistened as ours did minutes before. He cleared his throat. "I see there is agreement among you four. In that case, it is official." He raised his glass and we recited our charge in unison, "*Agite Excelsius!*"

We rushed to Leonardo's side and each shook his hand. It was official. Our new contract. The families and Lorenzo broke out into a standing applause and wild cheer.

We cleared the dishes and moved the tables and chairs aside. It was time for a celebration of singing and dancing, to finish off a fantastic evening. Giovanna's sister and Ben's brothers brought out their *lute*[48], recorder, tambourine, and drums. An evening of music, singing, and dancing began.

Giovanna pulled out her puppet Pulcino, and Leonardo his puppet, Fibonacci — two beautifully crafted birds of flight designed with fine motor movements of the head, feet, and wings under the artistic orchestration of their hands. They entertained Ben's two youngest

---

[48] Lute → A plucked stringed instrument with a long neck and a rounded body.

brothers with a game of Early Bird Gets the Worm using some of Momma's extra pasta noodles from dinner and grapes from dessert.

The kids got a kick out of the puppets playing with each other. Giovanna snacked on several grapes herself, which got Fibonacci a bit upset. Giovanna split up a few grapes and fed them to Fibonacci, making him very happy.

As the kids from all families played, I noticed Ben's father and Cristina's mother chatting a lot during the evening. I saw them share genuine smiles and heard laughs that made me believe something special was developing. It seemed that this apprenticeship created special friendships for me — lifelong friends who know not only who you are, but also the person you were and want to be. And now for others in our lives, our connection was bringing them together in a special way through a common interest, for them to possibly develop a special connection.

As the evening got late, Leonardo thanked the women for a wonderful dinner and my parents for hosting this gathering. Momma said he was welcome to dinner any time. Leonardo said he would try and take her up on the offer as she was a fabulous cook and made the best gnocchi he had ever had.

Leonardo worked his way around the yard, talking with them and thanking each family for a wonderful evening. He proceeded to where the four of us apprentices were chatting. "There was one item I wanted to mention to you. Seven months ago, there was a special delivery made out of town, which contained the secret crates along with confidential designs. I believe most of you were very interested back then and tried to check them out in the studio."

Ben answered with a warm, quiet laugh, "Yes, we had a deep, fallen interest in the subject. But unfortunately, we got distracted."

Leonardo continued, "Well, there have been some developments in this regard and I could use your expertise and assistance."

Cristina asked, "Is this the place near Paris?"

Leonardo smiled at us with an air of excitement and adventure. "Yes, at Château du Clos Lucé, in Amboise. Just a day's ride from Paris. Would you all like to go?"

We had been challenged by Codex Silenda, and with an impressive year of learning and adventure from a greater Master than I could ever imagine. This virtuoso extraordinaire introduced us to a world of creativity, artistry, and scientific wonder. He taught us to think outside the box into a world and universe of endless possibilities.

He heightened our sense of curiosity and quest for knowledge. We learned to collaborate in concert with our creative and logical thoughts. All with the goal to understand and enjoy the harmony and balance of life.

So when there arises an opportunity to explore the unbelievable, the magnificent, the mind-blowing, and the jaw-dropping within the far-reaching expanse and depths of the incredible, then by all means *carpe diem, quam minimum credula postero*[49]. Go for the ride of your life.

We were apprentices and explorers of the great Leonardo di ser Piero da Vinci. Ben, Cristina, Giovanna, and I looked at each other for a short second. We each shared adventurous grins and formed our quadrumvirate[50] artist handshake.

---

[49] *Carpe diem, quam minimum credula postero* → Latin for "Seize the day, put very little trust in tomorrow (the future)."

[50] Quadrumvirate → A group of four talented and awe-

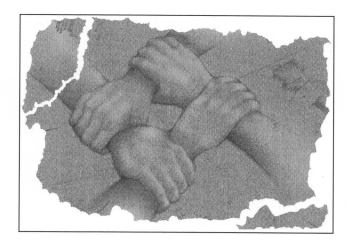

We were a team. In unison, we raised our hands upward and provided a resounding and unmistakable response: "YES!" We were in!

---

inspiring apprentices.

HEADLINE NEWS (PRESENT DAY)

Workers Rescued; Leonardo da Vinci Artifacts Found in Florence, Italy

FLORENCE, Italy (XBN Times, *in cooperation with IL PRAECO news-paper*) -- At a building construction site in downtown Florence, four site workers, who had been trapped for five hours in the early morning, were rescued and treated for hypothermia and exposure at a local medical facility.

Florence Police Chief, Silvia Romano, stated: "We are glad the workers are safe and we are now investigating to understand what happened. All work at the site has been halted. We are working with archaeologist Rubera Bostaurusini and her team to do an immediate analysis of a large object found at the site to ensure there are no immediate risks."

Bostaurusini was interviewed shortly after they performed the initial artifact examination. She stated, "This find is incredible. First, through initial forensic archaeological analysis, my team and I suspect the workers uncovered an old wooden cassone, a Renaissance-era marriage chest possibly be 500 to 600 years old. It was magnificently decorated and carefully preserved.

But, the chest was configured as some sort of specially-protected time capsule in the form of a 'Thieves' Snare', an elaborate puzzle, that we strongly believe was designed by the great Leonardo da Vinci. Unfortunately, as strange as this may seem, the 'snare' trapped the construction workers for several hours until my team was able to solve the puzzle."

"Second, from there we safely opened up the time capsule and discovered a large wooden book and several pages of paper scrolls, still intact, and in pristine condition. We believe the book is the Codex Silenda. My team also suspect this site was the location of Leonardo's studio during the late 1400's. The team is reviewing the scrolls now and will publish its findings soon."

"Earlier this year, we discovered the personal journals of Francesco Andrea Aiello, an apprentice of Leonardo da Vinci. The journals, written in early Florentine Italian, have been transcribed. Its contents describe Mr. Aiello's experiences with Leonardo da Vinci and … the Codex Silenda."

"Today's discovery may answer many questions that we and historians have been pursuing for decades. Our goal now is to closely examine the Codex Silenda book and possibly replicate it in exact detail for other scientists and academics to use as research."

"Based on Aiello's journals we first found, we knew the Codex Silenda existed but it was only described in those journals. We initiated a Kickstarter campaign after that discovery to help fund this venture. We exceeded our funding objectives in only six days! Now that we have an actual Codex Silenda book, we will probably further expand our funding. It will be exciting to see what happens next."

REVELATION, REFLECTION, AND BEAUTY

The day when Cristina injured her wrist working on her sculpture, we were each working on our own separate projects. Earlier that morning, Leonardo shared specific brush stroke techniques with us; we were to replicate what he had done. Ben and I worked on paintings while Cristina applied the techniques on clay.

Cristina had been working at her station for a while and stopped, holding her left wrist, "Ow!" Ben and I looked over, but continued our work. Cristina supported her wrist with the other hand and massaged it carefully. She winced with every touch on her wrist. Cristina walked over to a water bucket and wrapped her aching wrist in a cool, damp rag to help reduce the pain.

While on a break, she watched Leonardo sketch on the canvas. He picked up a mirror every so often and gazed into it. Then put it down and continued.

I glanced over and noticed he had outlined some of the components of a face; eyes, nose, mouth, face, and head. The drawing had facial contours and shading to show depth and character. I could not tell whose face it was, though it could have been a self-portrait.

Leonardo put down the charcoal and crossed his arms, looking at what he had drawn. He seemed bewildered; searching for something.

Leonardo looked out the window and then over to Cristina, who was holding her wrist carefully.

"You will be fine. Let your muscles rest for a bit."

Leonardo stood up and moved a chair to the right of his canvas.

"Come here, have a seat." Leonardo gestured to the chair.

Cristina sat down and relaxed her legs, placing her arms on the arm of the chair, while still caressing her wrist.

Standing in back of the chair, Leonardo placed his hands on her shoulders, "Sit up a bit. Turn your face a little to the left." He untied the bow holding her hair together. He straightened Cristina's hair and let it drape over her shoulders. He placed a light veil over her hair. "There."

Leonardo returned to his seat and picked up his pencil. He shared a smile with Cristina and continued working on the canvas. I leaned over and saw him sketch Cristina's upper torso, breast, shoulders, arms, and hands.

Leonardo called out to Ben and me, "You, too. Come over here."

We walked over to his station. Leonardo pointed back and forth between specific areas of the sketch and Cristina, "See the oval facial profile. Now the eyes, lips, nose. And the eyebrows and eyelids. The face is the most important part of any portrait. Focus on these features and the rest falls into place. This is the soul of a portrait. Where the spirit does not work with the hand there is no art." Ben and I followed Leonardo's explanation in detail.

Leonardo continued his sketch. "As artists, you have a certain artistic license you may exercise; call it leeway in your interpretation for how you reflect the subject of your drawing, sculpture, or whatever art. Think of it as freedom to produce art based on your personal insight."

Cristina removed the wet cloth from her wrist and placed it on the floor, still pampering her injury.

Leonardo gently called out, "Keep still. Back to how you were sitting, please." Leonardo smiled back at Cristina.

She returned the smile to him and snuck a glance at Ben and me with a grin of guiltiness and unexpected elation.

Leonardo continued working that morning, fine tuning the drawing. Ben and I returned to our projects, while Cristina worked on another activity, taking care of her wrist. Leonardo glanced over at Cristina every once in a while and made small adjustments in the drawing.

Afterwards, Leonardo retreated to his desk and took a well-needed nap. His passion and focus were exhausted early that day. The three of us spied a peek at the canvas and marveled at it for several minutes; each of us were totally speechless.

That morning, Cristina was a surprise subject as Ben and I watched Leonardo transform the majesty of Cristina and her inner beauty into a masterpiece. The portrait of Cristina is still fresh and vivid in my memory.

For Cristina, Ben, and me, this was just another extraordinary day as apprentices in the studio of Leonardo da Vinci.

ABOUT THE AUTHOR

Brad Jefferson lives in Sterling, Virginia with his wife. He enjoys writing, photography, and the great outdoors. His greatest achievement are his two grown children.

He strives to take advantage of every opportunity to meet people, enjoy nature, open new frontiers, and cherish the world around him.

Agite Excelsius!

Made in the USA
Middletown, DE
08 June 2019